A.D Stevens

The Jade Pandora

Lemma, The Star At The Beginning

A.D Stevens

Jay - "Bobbing and weaving trying to escape his Frilly Prison"

Me - "Wheat Sacks"

A.D Stevens

A.D Stevens

Copyright Page

The Jade Pandora: Lemma, The Star at the beginning

Cover Design by: Andrew Stevens (Author)

Interior Layout by: Andrew Stevens (Author)

ISBN: 9798264950308 (Paperback)

Published by: Independently published

For more information, Email:

A.D Stevens

Mr A Stevens – A.D_Stevens@outlook.com

Www.ad-stevens.co.uk

A.D Stevens

Acknowledgements

My Daughters, you are always a significant influence on me and how I try to live my life, so it is only right that I thank you and in the only way I can think of by adding you to one of my books.

My wife. I aimed to get this out for you, big 40, and since the main character is based on you and how I see you from my husband's point of view, it just made sense to celebrate you in this way.

Julia, once again, you have proven to be a great help in the editing process. I can not say thank you enough. Hopefully, you are ready for the next one.

A.D Stevens

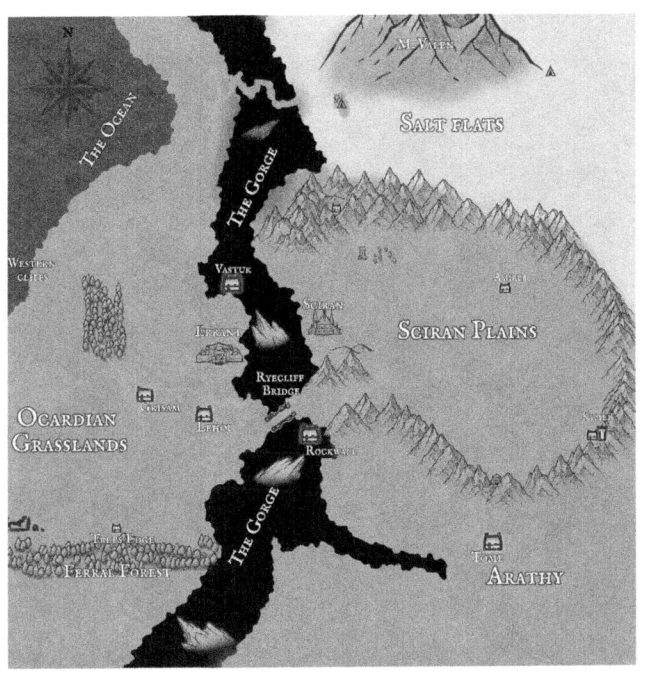

A.D Stevens

1

A Cousin's Plight

It started as any other day at the palace, where servants and attendants tried to do everything for her. Lemma hated it; she abhorred all the pomp and servitude that came from her being a princess of the realm. She would much rather do it all herself. Indeed, most of the time, she would. Unless her mum or sisters caught her, not letting the staff do their jobs. Rising from within her silken sheets, she pulled on a robe and crossed her bedchamber, gazing into the standing mirror placed just to the left of her door.

By Rysand, I can already hear the handmaidens in the other room prepping breakfast and my clothing. Can they not leave me alone? Pushing the door open, she heard the words she hated with a passion from the older of the two maids. "Princess, Breakfast is ready, or do you prefer to dress first?" Lemma's tongue beat her brain on this occasion, scolding them both. "I'd rather you just left me to my own devices."

"Apologies, your majesty, I did not mean any offence." Spoke the younger maid. "I'm sorry, girls, I woke on the wrong side of my bed. It's not personal." Lemma respectfully returned the apology, giving it some thought. I had better make friends; I don't need Mum or those nuisance sisters of mine finding out. Moving to the table, set with all manner of fruits and pastries, she sat down and began to eat a small orange, pressing it into a fluffy pastry. "Princess, which clothing do you wish us to fetch for today?" asked the maids in tandem.

Lemma spoke between bites, "Do either of you know if my Mother has anything planned for me today?" "I have been informed of no official duties for your attention today." Informed the older maid. "Then if you can, my armour, I intend to train with the priest guards." Retorted Lemma in a pleasant tone.

Breakfast finished, Lemma rose from the table, moving to the dressing area behind the ornate triple-fold screen, deftly decorated with scenes from the city and the plains beyond, the centre picture a vibrant tapestry depicting the Castle where she stood, in all its glory. White stone towers and spires touch the clouds, the rounded structure smooth and pristine. Grabbing her inner layer of leather from the top of the screen, she pulled the leather trousers up over her legs. Then she donned a tight Soutein-gorge before having the upper leather overcoat pulled over her outstretched arms above her head.

Stepping out of the covered area, Lemma buckled the iron shin and thigh guards, pulling the straps tight, then came back to standing. "Are you ready for the chest piece, Princess?" spoken by the older maid. "Ensure the fit, please, don't leave it loose." Arms outstretched, one maid held the armour in place, whilst the other deftly secured the rear armour in place via the leather straps. Finally, Lemma tightened the lower arm guards into place.

****

The daylight filled the training ground, and dust lifted into the air as boots scuffed about as those in attendance sparred with swords and daggers. Each member of the priest guard was covered in armour similar to Lemma's, the only difference being the cowls that covered their heads, hiding their faces. Lemma stood studying each man's movements. The way they fought was like dancing, with smooth movements that used the entirety of their bodies to bring the full weight of each attack to bear. One man stood out amongst all of them: Khrom Pallius. He stood easily a head above the rest of the guards and Lemma. He was the newest addition to the guard, a devout follower of Rysand and stalwart defender of Sciran. His assignment to the priest guard was no surprise to many, given his skill on the battlefield, which had earned him some renown.

Lemma had taken a liking to him, finding him an unusual challenge and a formidable fighter. Khrom had become her only training partner, and she stood at ten losses to eight wins. Today, Khrom, I pull back one loss, maybe two if I don't leave you bloodied and unconscious. Charging the field, leaping high into the air, wooden dagger in hand, Lemma crashed down, smashing the dagger into Khrom's undefended neck, sending him tumbling over himself to the ground. "That's ten to nine, Khrom, you should have been more aware." Lemma gleefully taunted him whilst waiting for his attack.

Dirt cascaded into the air, forcing a deep back step from Lemma. A sudden jump from his kneeling position saw Khrom swinging his wooden sabre-style sword from the left, as his body curled through the air, preventing Lemma from seeing the small, wooden Kuni blade in his right hand, sweeping up towards her middle. Ducking the Sabre, switching to an attacking stance, wrapping her own body around and under his left arm, prevented the Kuni from striking what could be considered a fatal blow, seeing it glance off her lower ribs.

Two-handed is it today? I can play that game as well. Deftly, Lemma pulled a wooden star from her waist, a representation of her actual, unique weapon. The Star of Sciran. A five-bladed star, crafted from incredibly sharp Kuni-style blades, controlled lightning and endowed Lemma with the unique abilities of wisdom and the power to see the very soul of her adversaries. It was, after all, a weapon of the Rysendar, a weapon forged at creation by Rysand himself, and had travelled down the female Royalty from Sciran, the first star wielder and founder of the nation ever since.

Wooden star in hand, she threw it, striking keenly in the channel between the front and rear of Khrom's chest plate. A vicious crack pierced the very air, pulling the attention of all the other priest guards to the embattled pair. "Gah, you got me good. That will be a few weeks of healing, but I'm not done yet, Princess," Khrom growled loudly. No, but my next move will see you finished. A thought flashed through her mind as she rounded Khrom's rear, sliding under his legs, punching straight upwards, connecting squarely with the centre of his groin.

Crumpling forward headfirst, his face smashed into the sandy floor of the arena. Screaming while rolling about, holding his wheat sacks, Lemma turned back and taunted. "Ten, ten, and that's what you get for leaving the Wheat sacks open." Then she walked away victorious, picking up the wooden star and asking all present. "Who's next?"

No other guards moved to fight or respond to Lemma's challenge. "I swear you lot have grown weak. What if you actually have to fight a creature of Rycore? Will you just run and hide your heads in the dirt?" None answered, all shying away, shame on their faces in the knowledge she was right.

Leaving the arena out into the lower ring of the city, a scream caught her ears. Is that Arrianna? Spinning, she looked for the source of the sound, but couldn't see anyone in distress, let alone her cousin. Just out of view came another scream, this time mixed with sobs and horror. "Guards, help! My purse!" That was Arrianna, I know it.

Rushing towards the sound, she quickly swept past people in the road, skimming the cobblestone structure, as if her feet barely touched the ground, almost as if she were flying. Ahead, the guards gathered surrounding a lone woman slumped against the white stone wall of a haberdashery. "Arrianna!" Lemma screamed as she saw her tears flowing, blood dripping from the slight nick to the side of her neck. Arrianna looked up with her red, sodden eyes, sniffling. "Lemma, help me please, the guards say they can not aid me. The man took my purse, my Mothers' ring was in there."

An enormous surge of emotion hit Lemma right in the chest: sadness, guilt and anger. In one foul sweep, she felt her cousin's pain, unable to process it in the moment she had. Screaming, she grabbed one of the assembled guards and slammed him against the haberdashery door, the force so hard that the door flew open, making her stumble and the guard fly from her hand. His armour screeched against the stone floor as he crashed further inside. Spinning around to face the other guards. "How dare you tell a member of a noble family you can't help them?"

A fresh-faced guard drew his sword, lunging at Lemma. His first mistake was made as she pulled a small blade from her waist and hooked its loop around her index finger, twirling to his right-hand side as his blade sailed past. Slicing cleanly through the guard's leather armour and cutting deep into his upper thigh, dropping him to the floor as he yelled out in pain.

"Is this guard an utter mud muncher!?" came the cry from a senior officer as she ran, seeing Lemma's sudden arrival. The three Remaining guards stood to attention. "Corporal Nyrina, Mam." Each guard shot to attention and called their name. Nyrina stopped a single step away from the guard, still writhing on the floor, looking down on him. A swift kick to his head, seeing him fall silent. "You bunch of absolute Salt weasels, you let this mud muncher bear a blade at the princess!?" The enormity of the situation dawned on the three guards as they looked at Lemma, who stood steps away, her eyes fixed in absolute rage, focused solely on them.

Arrianna finally stood speaking with Lemma. "Cousin, he took my mother's ring, the last thing of hers I had. Please, you must help me see it returned." "Fantastic, you clueless idiot. Not only did you let him attack the princess, but you also ignored the pleas of her cousin." Nyrina stood ripping into the guards, but her thoughts didn't match. You're lucky to be alive right now, wheat sacks. The paperwork would be easier if you weren't.

Lemma stood, her emotions still surging as she spoke. "Tell me what this absolute degenerate of a thief looked like! Any detail, Arrianna will help. I will find Aunt Maggie's ring. No person will stop me." "He was about my height in a ragged set of cotton clothes. I can't forget that face. He placed his lips on my cheek as he sliced my neck." Through broken words, Arrianna spoke more. "His left eye was nothing but a scar, his right a dark, blackened red. A scar ran the length of his nose and his mouth." Arrianna retched at the thought. Those lips felt like poison on my cheek.

Arrianna's following words came forth with bile. "His lips were swollen, purple and cracked, rough and dry; it felt like they cut into my skin." "Corporal, you heard the description. Why are you still standing here?" Snapped lemma. Nyrina stood to attention. "I offer no excuse, my princess. I will see this man found." Shaking her head, Lemma spoke again, "You will not, I will. You will be by my side until I do, or else those guards will see the punishment my mother would demand."

"As you wish, my princess. Get your mud munching arses out of here and take that salt weasel with you. This never happened." Scolded Nyrina at the guards, still motionless and silent. Nyrina then sighed, thinking. Thank god I escaped the paperwork. Princess, you are an angel.

"Arrianna, head home. I will see to this, but first, I need the Star of Sciran." Arrianna took her leave, thanking Lemma.

"Princess, please just call me Nyrina, not by my rank. I do not deserve that honour currently." "Then, in that case, Nyrina, stop with the formality and call me Lemma while you work with me. Now to the castle first." Nyrina followed a couple of steps behind as they made for the castle.

2

Tracking Evil

In the castle, Lemma walked to the royal armoury, with Nyrina following behind. Lemma spoke, "Once I have the Star, we will return. Do not expect me to be nice. You hurt my family, I will hurt you." Said with malice to the air. Nyrina heard it even though she shouldn't have. I pity the man who has angered you.

The Royal Armoury stood before them, guards on either side of the two doors constructed from solid, silver trident metal. "Open up," Lemma ordered. Stepping into the centre, the guards both placed a red meridian key in the slots. "On my count…. Three… two… one." The keys turned in unison, and a giant bolt dropped, clunking away from where it was held to keep the door barred. The more senior guard moved to the centre, both hands on a large wheel, turning it counterclockwise and walking backwards, opening the vault door.

Striding forward past the guard, still pulling the door wide, Lemma entered the vault. There, at its centre on a pedestal, the Star of Sciran displayed in all its glory. *By Rysand, that Star is indeed shown off, even when sealed away.* Nyrina winced in its presence. Retrieving the Star and fastening it at her waist, Lemma stepped back out of the vault. "Seal it!" The senior guard grunted in acknowledgement as he shoved hard against the door to move it inward again. Once it closed, both guards turned the keys again, hearing the bolts click back into place, sealing the door closed.

****

Back in the outer ring, standing in front of the haberdashery again, the unconscious guard was still flat on his back inside the shop. Lemma entered, stepping over the guard, calling out, "Shopkeeper." A petite, old lady wrapped in a knitted shawl peered from behind the counter, her eyeglasses sitting on the tip of her nose. An almost silent squeaking voice sounding "How may I…" Her words stunted, gazing on Lemma. "Princess, to what does little old me do that deserves such a fortunate visit?" "My good lady, I'm here for the wrong reasons, but do not worry, it is not anything you have done. Did you witness the attack outside your shop earlier?" Lemma asked deliberately.

A noise came from outside the shop just as the old lady began to speak, drawing all attention to the door and the street beyond. Turning to step out the door, Lemma ordered. "Nyrina, you talk with this fine shopkeeper. I'll check on the commotion." "By your command, Lemma." Nyrina said with much apprehension after Lemma had stepped out. *That didn't feel very good to me, but that's what the princess asked for; I'd better get used to it.*

In the gutter of the Cobblestones stood a group of patrolmen. Harassing a young boy, approximately nine or ten years old. Six of them. Shouting and shoving the poor child about like a rag doll, demanding what little coin he gripped tight within his tiny hands. The Star had begun to glow a golden colour, pulsating at Lemma's waist, hooked to her right side. *Their souls are twisted. Not much, but enough for the Star to react. I must do something.*

Springing to the centre of the group. "Men, stop doing this. I, your Princess, command it." Her words hit an invisible wall; none of the six stopped at all. *I didn't want to use force, but if I must. I must.* Crouching low to the ground, Lemma placed her right leg out in front, left one bent tucked under her rear. She removed the Star from her waist with her right hand, pulling it up behind her, ready to throw. Dispatched from her hand, it shone as it rotated counterclockwise, a fine mist spreading from its surface as it separated the very air itself.

In a blink, the first guard went down, his Achilles tendon

severed, rendering him unable to stand. A swift look and the second guard crumpled to the ground, the rear of his knees slashed through, spurting blood covering the cobblestones. A sudden switch in orientation, the Star flew vertically over the head of the third guard, to crash back down. Slamming into the side of his helmet, the crunching metal folded in on itself, blinding the guard's right eye. A second impact slammed him into the nearest wall, his armour scraping as he slid to the ground out cold.

My turn, I think, Rysand, keep me safe. Leaping from her crouched position, Lemma swung her left elbow up into the base of the guard's unprotected nose. As it splintered and exploded, blood drenched his face and spurted out over Lemma's chest plate. He staggered backwards, screaming in agony. Lemma landed, sweeping herself round, taking the guard's legs from under him, sending him smashing to the ground.

The two remaining guards finally reacted, swords drawn, they moved together, one slashing from right to left, the other bringing his sword down from above. Lemma slung the dagger from her waist, forward into the first of the guards. The dagger deflected away, stunning him in place as the Star cut low under his sword arm, ripping through his tunic, cutting deep into the bicep, rendering the arm useless.

From nowhere, it seemed Khrom arrived. His size being used to his advantage, he hooked under the final guard's arms from behind, lifting him clear off the floor and leaving his legs flailing about as he thrashed to further his attack. "My gods, Princess, what did they do to deserve this? I'm glad I have never been unfortunate enough to fight you when you wield the Star." Khrom's voice took on an air of fear.

"Would you calm down, man, that's the princess, do you not see her?" Khrom demanded of the guard, still fighting in his arms. No response, just continued struggles and attempts to flee. Khrom sighed, "Oh, whatever you mud muncher, you can't hear me, can you?" Dropping the guard and bringing both fists with all his might into each side of his head in one almighty blow, then watching as the guard flopped forward, face-planting into the cobblestone.

The Star back in Lemma's hand had calmed itself, and the glow faded, easing the air around her. Two of the guards were silent and still, the remaining four releasing vicious and angry cries of pain. Lemma moved to the one whose ankles would most likely never see him walk again and spoke, "I see you have a clear mind; the taint is gone. Why did you attack the child?"

Delirious and holding both ankles, stemming the bleeding as best he could, the patrolman looked up, "Princess, where am I!? What child!? Last I remember, I was trying to apprehend a man with one eye." The other guards had finally begun to reclaim their minds, and through their pain echoed the first man's words.

"Khrom send for men to help these souls while I gather

information," Lemma ordered, turning back to the first patrolman. "A man with one eye, where? Describe him, was it his left eye?" Nyrina exited the shop after speaking with the old lady, who revealed that the attacker had fled directly from the store towards the middle ring. "What in all Apprite!" she exclaimed, seeing all of the Patrolmen lying about, covering the valleys between white cobbles of the street, crimson red from their wounds. "Nyrina, the thief, these men tried to arrest him." Caught off guard by Lemma's words, Nyrina questioned, "Where, princess?"

Khrom returned with members of the priest guard, swiftly nodding to Lemma and speaking in a stunted manner. "Ny…rina, why are you here?" A flash of pink filled his cheeks on seeing Nyrina. "You look wonderful this day, Corporal." Nyrina stood in silence, blushing at his words, without realising it, pushing strands of her blemished blonde hair from over her eye to reveal sand coloured eyes staring back at Khrom. "Will you two get a room or get it together and help me. Nyrina, princess!? Really?" "Sorry, Lemma, it's all too fresh, I'm not used to being so informal."

The other members of the priest guards had stretchered away the patrolmen, and the guard who had remained silent throughout the entire fight from the shopkeeper's floor. Lemma had told Khrom and Nyrina to go on ahead of her, with instructions to speak with the citizenry for information on the thief.

Nyrina had gathered a small amount of information about a

dishevelled man. The men she had spoken to had seen him take flight down a dark alley into the shadows, then disappear from view; none had seen him exit. Lemma and her cohorts tracked the thief through the alley, its mud; they saw footprints, fresh and deep. "Someone moving fast recently passed here," Nyrina said, kneeling next to the fourth set they had come across. Perturbed Khrom chimed in, "To where did he flee? This alley is a dead end." As he pulled the lid from a wooden crate strewn along the alley walls. "Nope, not hiding in here", swore Khrom. *You truly know how to make yourself look like a dumb ass salt weasel.* Lemma chuckled at her own thoughts whilst focusing on her surroundings.

This is useless; there is nothing here. Frustrated, Lemma kicked the ground at her feet. The twang of metal meeting metal toe cap rang back at her. *What was that?* Kicking the floor again, the ting of metal on metal. "Khrom here, there's something on the floor." Kneeling by Lemma, Khrom ran his fingers through the wet, sludgy mud, tracing the metallic frame and eventually catching his fingers on a notch-like handle. Lifting with his right arm, a metal hatch opened, revealing a dark, sullen staircase.

"Fetch torches, commandeer them from the street lighters if needs be." Nyrina sprinted from the alley at Lemma's order. "On it, Lemma, be back swiftly." She called over her shoulder, running for the main street.

3

Dinner Below The City

Torches in hand, they began their descent into the muck and shadow beneath the city. Few had ever walked those depths; most knew of them only through rumour and half-forgotten tale. It was said the place was not built by the city, nor by royalty, but by older hands to bury the tainted, the damned, and the things best left unseen—the tunnels wound beneath every ring of the city like roots beneath a dying tree.

The final step left them with a thrown-together wooden door, through which a faint light could be seen —the flickering of a flame, dancing somewhere behind it. Khrom slowly lifted the door's iron latch, then edged it open, looking through the gap it formed. "I see no movement." "Open the door then, so we can all enter." Lemma hissed in a low whisper. *I want that thief, and your caution slows me too much.*

Khrom led the way, followed by the others, into a large stone-built tunnel, lit only enough for them to see the path ahead. *Incredibly well-built, these walls and supports look solid,* Khrom noted. They moved in a triangular pattern, with two facing forward and one to the rear, used to keep all areas in sight. Each of them held a weapon, fixed and ready to attack if needed.

Lemma spoke quietly to the others. "I smell food, and it smells good." The smell wafted from in front of them, and they were unsure whether it came from behind the door they approached or from the tunnel opposite, which led deeper into the maze of tunnels. Nyrina remarked on the smell, then spoke. "We should clear the room first, Lemma, then move on from there." "Agreed." Nodded Lemma in return. Lifting the lock on the door directly to her left, Lemma eased the door open a fraction.

Inside the room, the faintest of glows caught their eyes as they entered. The star shone bright, hinting at an evil in this room. "Hold, do not move." Lemma hushed them as she ordered, using the light of the star to check the room thoroughly. In the far corner, from which the first light they saw originated, something caught her eye. Khrom pushed in front of Lemma, placing her at his back.

"What is that, Princess? It looks like no man or beast?" Casting the star out into the room, spinning to the far wall, and ricocheting to the right-hand side of the room, again bouncing and returning to Lemma's hand.

Having taken the chance to gaze into the body's soul, only to find the lack of one, Lemma explained. "It's a man, yet not. The body seems empty, devoid of life; only the slightest taint of Rycore remains. Just a dusty husk." The light was just the final remnant of a coal burning at the body's feet. Aghast and horrified, Nyrina retreated from the room, unable to reconcile the scent of mould and wetness with the shrivelled, blackened remains within. "Rysand watch over us", she whispered. *This is what the priests guard do; it's not my concern. I'm just a simple army corporal, yet the princess dragged me along.*

Exiting the room, Khrom and Lemma walked into another dimly lit tunnel that stretched out before them. At the farthest end, a brighter, more vibrant light shone. They moved back into their position before continuing. To Lemma's mind, they had moved about halfway to the light when they heard voices from the other side of the wall. "Hush, quiet, I hear someone. I think there's a room on the other side of this wall. Listen."

Silently, they all stood listening. From behind the wall came a man's voice, muffled but clear enough to make out the words. "Gruladan has done it now, he attacked a relative of the crown, the Princess hunts him personally." *Gruladan, did I hear that right? So, finally, a name for this one-eyed thief.* Indicating the need to move on, Lemma led them towards the room at the end of the tunnel, stopping short of the door. Lemma whispered instructions, "The star senses nothing, so anyone beyond is man alone; if they attack, they are for you to deal with." Khrom and Nyrina nodded and moved to the door, bursting into the room.

"It's a mud munching kitchen, no wonder the tunnel smelt so good," Khrom exclaimed, seeing nobody in the room. Over a fire pit in the centre hung a massive cast iron pot full to near its brim with food bubbling away. "Smells like repeaters stew", Nyrina added once she too had made sure the room was empty. "Repeater stew? What is that!?" Lemma didn't have a clue what it was, simply because she had never been served it. "Lemma, repeaters stew is a poor man's meal; the pot never empties. That way it always stays flavourful and ready to be eaten." Nyrina explained. *I haven't had a bowl of repeaters stew in forever, since before I joined the army, I think.* Fond memories of childhood filled Nyrina's mind. Without realising it, she had gravitated to the pot, grabbed the ladle, and brought it to her lips.

"Nyrina, what are you doing, dammit?" Lemma scolded across the room rather loudly. Nyrina dropped the ladle. "Err… erm, I don't know, the smell captivated me, I haven't eaten since morning, sorry." Shaking her head, Lemma returned Nyrina's gaze. "Just eat, can't expect you to fight on an empty stomach. In fact, could you make me a bowl? Khrom, you keep watch. If you want to, eat after us." Khrom chuckled under his breath. "For all that is Rysand, you chose now of all times to eat, I just couldn't write this." "What was that, Khrom?" "Nothing, princess, just thinking out loud that I could eat a bowl too."

Lemma and Nyrina took bowls from a rough, carved shelf in the stone walls. Nyrina served a portion to both as Lemma commented. "If that actually tastes half as good as it smells, I'll be asking the castle kitchen to make it." Nyrina's face creased up, holding back laughter. *Repeaters stew from the castle kitchen, well, I never.* "Are you two finished yet? My stomach is going nuts over here." Asked Khrom aggressively. "Yes, let me switch with you," Nyrina replied. "You ate that quickly, Nyrina. I can see why. It tastes pretty darn good, actually." Lemma said with a content smile, going back for seconds

Once the party had eaten their fill of the stew, they returned to exploring the tunnels. Leaving the kitchen on its far side, they entered another tunnel, leading to another big room full of wooden furniture. Entering, they discovered several people. Instantly, one of the men in the room attacked, having spotted them. They launched chairs through the air, aiming for Khrom, the tallest of the bunch. Khrom deftly dodged the bulk, slicing the ones he couldn't in half with his sabre. Distracted by Khrom, the aggressors had not noticed that Nyrina and Lemma had split to either side of the room, encircling to the rear.

Nyrina made the first move, swiftly thrusting her straight sword into the rear end of the nearest man, slicing the deep and shallow femoral arteries, dropping him dead to the floor. Blood sprayed out, covering the length of her sword and all over her chest plate. Only one thought entered her head. *I never knew you could kill a man by ramming something in their arse.* Lemma had pounced in the confusion, using her Kuni dagger and slashing her nearest assailant's throat from behind.

The gurgled sound of his final words alerted the other to their presence as his heart pumped the last sprays of crimson from his severed jugular all over them and the smooth stone floor. Three men ran forward, two toward Nyrina and one toward Lemma, while the remaining three continued pelting Khrom with furniture from the other side of the room.

The two men running at Nyrina overlooked the pool of blood around her from the man she had already dropped. Miss stepping into it, their feet lost traction on the bloodied stone. The axe in one man's hand, carved deep into the ribs of the other, cracking them wide open in the chaos, as he slid directly onto the point of Nyrina's sword. Impaled straight through the larynx, the light faded from his eyes, bloodied gasps spluttering from his parted lips as he took his last breath. Curtailing her laughter, Nyrina cast the man to the floor, thinking, *By Rysand, that was easier than expected. I didn't do anything.*

The Star at the begining

The attacker rushing at Lemma jumped onto a table, diving with his sword outstretched, trying to skewer her through the chest. Lemma side-stepped as the man sailed past her, smashing to the floor and breaking his nose. *Oh, lovely, were those teeth flying away from him?* Jumping on the man's back, pinning him, "Where is Gruladan? Tell me, and you may yet live." The man, unable to form proper words, mumbled. " Th… the… Trea…ure. Cham…ber." "Where is that?" Lemma asked again. The man didn't answer, lying there unconscious from his injuries. *Oh, wheat sacks, why couldn't he hang on only a second longer?*

Unfortunately for the three who still flung furniture at Khrom, he'd had enough of this merry dance dodging and diving from the projectiles. *Okay, I'm done. Forgive me, Rysand, for what I am about to do.* Tearing a leg from one of the shattered Tables, he threw it with great force, its point wedging and burying deep into the forehead of the centre man, sending him flying back, crashing into the wall behind him. Dead. Blood and clear liquid leaked from the sides of the table leg, now protruding from his skull. The other two men, fearing for their lives, dropped the furniture they were holding and the weapons attached to their waists, realising they were outnumbered. Khrom moved to the now still assailants, a vile scent hit him in the nostrils. "What on Apprite, it smells like Mullock dung…" His words cut off as he choked on the vile vapours, thinking. *Did he just fertilise his own field?* Khrom shook his head in disgust and spoke to the man in front of him.

"A sage choice, my friend. Now, if you wish to live much longer, give us the information Princess Lemma requires." Khrom barked in the face of one of the men while holding him by the throat, dangling him off the floor. The other man sat on the floor cross-legged, arms above his head, Nyrina's sword at his throat, silent.

Choking, the man spoke. "Information, yes, what information?" Lemma stepped forward. "Gruladan, where is he?" The man's eyes widened, realising why he was in this predicament. "We all told him not to do it. To return the ring. Princess, he wouldn't listen, took it to the treasure room." Lemma smiled faintly, a glint in her eye. *I'm close, Gruladan. I'm coming for you. You will be captured.*

"How do I get to the treasure room from here?" Lemma snarled at the man, "Hurry, answer, my patience wears thin." "Through the door on the right, then right again. Enter the storage room, which should be empty of people. Exit it at the rear. The next room will be the armoury, and more men will likely be there. After the armoury, left, then right, and you'll be there, princess." Khrom smacked the man in the side of the head and tossed him to the ground. *You still breathe, be happy,* he thought as the man's head bounced off the stone floor.

Nyrina smashed the pommel of her sword into the man's

temple, who was still sitting cross-legged under her sword's tip, sending him crashing to the floor out cold, with no light left in his eyes. "That door over there", Nyrina indicated with her sword outstretched before sheathing it.

It had been smooth sailing; the armoury was empty, having made it to the treasure room following the directions they had been given. Standing by the door listening, a single voice came from the room. "That idiot Gruladan, this is a royal ring. Why would he bring it here? The whole army will be looking for this." Lemma slammed the door open, sending it swinging so hard that the hinges snapped, sending it crashing to the floor in front of its opening.

Inside the room, a lone old man stood behind a desk full of ledgers and parchments, covered in numbers and sums. His face was covered with a grey beard that reached the top of his chest; the hair on his head was dark, dreary, and thin. A bald patch at the centre reflected the torches that lit the room on its surface. Stuttering, he spoke, "Prin... Princess...Ho...How...Deli...Delight.... Full... To...See...You... I.. Ha...Have.. The...Ring...You...See...Seek... Here."

"Good, I am glad you see sense, sir. Hand it over, and those ledgers, I might add. Proof of your crimes and ill-got gains, I expect!" Lemma demanded. "Not my gains, your highness. I'm just the banker for these rotten Mud munchers who call this underground home." The man added as quickly as he could in his own defence.

"Khrom, fetch the ring and those ledgers. Nyrina, you will be this man's guard as he takes us back to the surface and then his interviewer for Gruladan's whereabouts." Lemma's orders came across curt and short; her anger at not finding Gruladan was immense and filled the air. "Gruladan, your highness, he will no doubt be at the Rising Sun this evening, partaking of the ale and ladies." The man offered up in the hope that it would lighten his sentence. "Thank you, sir, you seem to be wise, and for your honesty, I will pass sentence now. Three days in the stocks, but I warn you, the army will take the underground; any attempt to return or further crimes will be met with fierce punishment."

A smile formed on the old man's face. "Thank you for such mercy, your majesty. I will not forget your word and find an honest way to feed my family."

4

Story Time

With the surface came the light piercing their eyes, forcing each to squint and stand stunned until their eyes had adjusted. "It's Morning, How?" Nyrina spoke the words but couldn't understand herself. The old man chimed in. "The tunnels have a habit of messing with your perception of time; hours can seem like mere minutes."

"Nyrina, take him to the stocks, then join me in the castle. I'll leave word with Barret to expect you; your work deserves a reward. The royal baths? Khrom, head back to the barracks. You will be rewarded, but I've yet to decide how." "By your leave, Highness",

Khrom answered and passed the ring and ledgers to Lemma. Nyrina nervously answered. "Erm, don't know what to say, Lemma. The royal baths? I'm not worthy, the stories make them sound heavenly," before forcing the old man to march towards the middle ring of the city.

****

"Mother dearest, I have reclaimed Arriana's ring and shattered the criminal underbelly of the city. By myself, might I add. The army has been instructed to map and clear the underground." "Lemma, you impudent child! How could you put yourself at such risk and make such a mess in the lower ring? Those patrolmen you maimed have been compensated and sworn to secrecy over their involvement. Your sister Isis dealt with it very delicately; the patrolmen dared not speak for their shame of being tainted!" Catherine screamed at Lemma from the throne. *By Rysand, some days, daughter of mine, I swear I could strangle you.*

"But Mother, I am safe, you can see that." A disconcerting tone just on the edge of Lemma's words. "Well, anyway, the city's criminals have nowhere to hide, and tonight I will capture the one who escaped me and dared to raise a blade to a member of our family. I need not have those feelings again", Lemma spoke extra earnestly to assuage Catherine's fears and anger. *It was like Arrianna was the one driving me; it wasn't nice, like my feelings weren't my own.*

"You don't understand, do you? My Child, you are still

young, and you are the one chosen by the Star to take the throne after me. Why do you insist on running amok among the people? You are this city's— no, this country's future." Still full of anger, Catherine slammed her hand down on the throne's arm. *I can not fathom for the life of me where you get this rebellious attitude from.*

Lemma turned to her side, rolling her eyes as she explained, "I'm Sorry, mother, it was like I was possessed. I had to aid Arrianna; my mind couldn't settle, nor has it settled, because of this man Gruladan." Lemma insisted, unmoving. "I suppose you have always been more attuned to others than most, even in your early years; you would sob for no reason if one of your sisters even skinned a knee. Fine, capture this man, and that will be the end of it, I hope" Catherine, firm in her stance, glared down at Lemma from the throne. "Yes, mother, it will," Lemma reassured Catherine with a beaming smile. *Well, it will be once I've gotten my hands on him.*

In the Royal Baths, Lemma stood wrapped in a pure white, thousand-thread towel made by the city's finest silk-smith, waiting patiently for the red-faced and bashful Nyrina, who still hadn't dared to remove her outer armour for fear of Lemma laughing at her naked form. "Get undressed, Ny, we both have the same bits, given I think yours may actually dwarf mine." A slight curl appeared at the edges of Lemma's lips as she said this. "Forgive me, Lemma. I'm used to bathing alone; I'm the only woman in my unit." Nyrina replied, turning her face away, trying to hide her shyness. *By the gods' ill strip you myself, if I have to, I want to get in the bath.*

Before Lemma's thought had fully passed through her head, her hand had acted, grasping Nyrina's chest plate straps, undoing them, and ripping it from over Nyrina's head. "See, not that difficult, come on, the water's fine and waiting."

Unclipping the rest of the armour from her leathers, Nyrina undressed. She removed her Leather tunic to reveal her olive-toned skin and slim figure. "I knew you were strapping them down." Lemma squealed, seeing Nyrina's chest wrapped in bandages. *Now I get to play, I'll have you giggling in no time.* Launching at Nyrina, leaving her own towel to fall to the bath house floor, exposing her hourglass body and her own firmer olive tanned skin

Next, snatching the loose tail of the bandage, tugging at it with glee. Lemma watched as Nyrina spun on the spot, laughing, letting her more girlish spirit show. One never seen by people outside of the castle, *why am I so comfortable with Nyrina, I wonder?* Slowly, the bandages unwound, revealing Nyrina's Wheat hills. "In all that is Rysand, those things are weapons you could knock a Mullock out with them." Nyrina shot towards the floor, crouching, curling her arms around her knees, hiding behind her own legs, her olive skin now a braised glow of pink, red, and crimson. "Please, Princess, stop teasing me." *This is why I bathe alone.*

Lemma couldn't help herself as she continued to stare and taunt her. *I don't remember the last time I had this much fun.* Casting the final parts of the bandage to the floor, swooping behind Nyrina. Smack, the sound of Lemma's hand slapping on the bare skin of Nyrina's backside. The shock hit Nyrina hard, launching her forward above her. The sound of the slap echoed in the changing room, quickly followed by a high-pitched scream and full-bellied laughter. Sprawled out face-first on the floor, Nyrina lay there, her eyes pinned and focused in disbelief as Lemma squealed through laughter. "That's for calling me princess."

Dashing forward, planting legs on either side of Nyrina's back, sitting on her, reaching down at her side. Lemma lightly danced her fingertips across Nyrina's skin under her armpits. Through the throes of ever-heightening laughter, Lemma said, "Say it! Say I'm Beautiful!" "Stop it! I can't take it. I submit, you win. I'm beautiful…I admit it, I'm beautiful." Nyrina screamed as her body bucked around, shedding tears in laughter, and throwing Lemma all over as she tried to escape Lemma's impromptu tickle assault. "Lemma, please, I beg, I can't hold my bladder much longer."

Lemma released her. "Now, can we bathe? Are you willing to accept me? I wish you to be my friend, Ny" Nyrina dragged herself up from the floor. *I've seen how you treat your enemies, and now I know how you treat your friends. Wheat sacks, what else am I in for?* "Yes, Lemma, I see you treat me differently from the other soldiers. Friends, it is then", Nyrina replied with a full smile.

Lemma grabbed Nyrina's hands, pulling her along and down

the steps into the royal bath, flopping onto her back and letting herself float. "Join me, relax, this is your reward, but my friend..." A degree of cheekiness in her words before Nyrina cut her off, "My friend, what Lemma?" Nyrina asked apprehensively. "Oh, nothing, Ny, just you'll be getting a royal dinner as well." Ny? *When did I get a flaming nickname? Hey, it might be good to have the princess at my back; might as well make the most of it.* Her thoughts melted away as she let herself float on the surface of the bath with Lemma.

The bells tolled outside, signalling the fourth hour of the afternoon. Still, Lemma and Nyrina floated in the bath, the scent of lavender and orange seeped into their skin, the brush of pumice stones grazing against them, revealing smooth, unblemished skin. Standing to the side of the bath, an attendant tried to signal Lemma, waving her arms above her head until Nyrina floated over and saw her.

Alarmed by the attendant's presence, she lurched to standing, splashing water in a small wave over Lemma's face. Choking as water filled her mouth, Lemma turned, seeing Nyrina shielding her modesty… again. "Princess, Dinner is served on the balcony," the attendant called. Lemma nodded in acknowledgement. "Ny, come on, we need to dress. The food is ready, oh, and by the way, I sent your armour to be cleaned, a nice slim dress is waiting for you." *I reckon you will work to keep the men away from me in it as well.* The unsaid words, Lemma thought.

Making their way from the bath together, Nyrina walked in a very awkward manner, right arm covering her chest, left hand covering her seed patch. "Ny, will you please be more confident? It's just me and you." Lemma questioned, looking at Nyrina's predicament. "Ok, Lemma, do you swear no man will enter. I wish to hide my form and keep their respect." Lemma spoke in surprise. "What did you think? No man would dare enter these Royal Baths, a place for the female royals only. They've got their own. So don't be silly, Ny, it's completely safe."

****

Dressed in flowing gowns, both of them looked at each other. "Lemma, that dress fits you so well, I doubt you will dare be in public for all the looks you'll get." Nyrina getting her compliment in first to receive a sudden compliment in return. "Ny, I pale in comparison to you. No man will look upon me with you by my side. I'd even say I'd manage to avoid proposals, as they would prefer to flirt with you." Lemma paused, taking in Nyrina's womanly form and gasped. "Wow, your figure, you shouldn't hide it at all." Nyrina's face turned blood red as she gazed at the floor, shyly trying to avoid eye contact with Lemma, her mind filled with strange thoughts. *Why did I like her complimenting me so much?"*

They sat at a small two-person wooden table on the balcony, ready to eat the meal placed before them. Nyrina's cheeks still flushed red as she digested Lemma's words. *Am I really as good as she says? Do I truly let myself be seen?* Placed before them were plates full of meat and fruit prepared in the royal kitchen, the smells of spices wafting under their noses. "Eat, Ny. I had it prepared for us." Taking a fork from the table, Lemma began to plate her own meal. "Lemma, if I may be so bold, can you tell me how the Star became yours?" Nyrina asked as she took a chunk of meat from the plate.

"Ny, honestly, why would there be an issue? I'm happy to tell you how I became the holder of the Star. First, though, you need to know how it works into the very fabric of our country." *Is it really that ingrained?* Nyrina wondered, smiling as she listened. "To start with, the city and country's namesake held the Star in the war of creation. Sciran, whose last name is unknown, and I don't think anyone bothered to write it down at the time. It then had to be passed down the female line only, hence why we always have a Queen. I will be next on the throne as its holder." *I wish I weren't, but I have to be for my people.* "My mother and grandmother were before me."

Nyrina jumped in. "Oh, I'd never even considered that we only ever had Queens, unlike other places, passing the throne to the firstborn son." Lemma chuckled, seeing the realisation spread across Nyrina's face. "So anyway, when the Queen gives birth to heirs, she will retain the power until usually the fifth birthday of the female heir; this isn't always the firstborn female. I'm the third born, so mum controlled the Star until about fifteen years ago; it skipped Isis and Faith, no idea why."

Confusion crossed Nyrina's face as she asked. "What if only male heirs are born?" Lemma stumped, stuttered slightly in her answer, "Err, never considered it. It's never happened, as if Rysand makes sure the new heir is always born. Some brainy scholars somewhere have speculated it's actually the soul of Sciran lying dormant inside the heir and comes forward to receive the Star like she is reborn each time." *If she is, I don't feel like another woman is inside me.* "I don't see how that can be, since both mum and I were around at the same time for at least the five years." Nyrina sat there dumbstruck. *Two people, one Star? At the same time, this is making my head hurt.* A realisation flooded Nyrina's mind, making her blurt out. "So princesses Isis and Faith failed the tests and can never be Queen!"

Lemma sat silently, shaking her head in disbelief. *Has that fact just really sunk in? I already said that I'm the next Queen. Well, at least I know you're listening.* A slight laugh escaped her lips, prompting a question from Nyrina, "What did I do? Why am I being laughed at?" "Oh, Ny, I wasn't laughing at you, more for the fact that you had the delayed reaction. I hope I didn't offend." Nyrina just shook her head to indicate she had taken no offence.

A very young servant girl moved to the table's edge, salivating at the rich and succulent meats at its centre. *I see you, I know I shouldn't, but you're just too cute.* "Shhh, here, young one, eat.

Don't let Barrett know I slipped it to you", Lemma said, smiling as she handed the girl a large slice of seared Mullock. The servant girl quickly devoured the meat, savouring its rich flavours. Whispering almost silently, "Thank you, Princess." Finished with the meat, the servant girl took the plate from the table and disappeared from the balcony.

Around five minutes later, the girl returned, pushing a dessert trolley bursting with cakes and all manner of delicate desserts. "Lemma, can I truly partake in these? They look too good for the likes of me." Nyrina said, feeling the pressure of sitting at a royal table. "I say it's ok, so it's ok. Ny, don't worry." *God's! Will you stop with the formality and enjoy it?* "Anyway, let's continue to eat. I need to finish the story" Lemma spoke, eager to continue. *It's so lovely to have someone to talk to who's closer to my age, for once, and who's interested in me, not my title.* "So anyway, that's enough of the history, I'm sure you get it. skipping forward to my fifth birthday." Lemma paused, biting into an elegant, heavily decorated plum sponge before speaking again.

"On my fifth birthday, I was taken to the arena in the lowest ring by mum to test if I was the next to receive the Star. To say the test is scary doesn't do it justice. I was at the height of this chair, maybe, unaware of what was going to happen. In the arena, all I could see were giants covered in metal, smashing each other with all types of weapons, even dodging arrows. I was in awe of it. Still, then I found out what the test was."

Nyrina didn't know what to say, so she just spewed out a string of words. "The test was scary, watching the metal giants wasn't? What could be worse than them?" Lemma smirked to herself. *Give me a chance to tell you.* "Yep, the test was simple. Mum would throw the Star at me with full power. If it stopped and fell into my hand, I was the next heir; if it passed me by, I wasn't." "What on Apprite!? The Queen threw the Star at you!?" Nyrina exclaimed.

"Indeed, she did so without a warning and without a care. Though she didn't expect the outcome she got. It still makes her laugh now. I stood there, staring at the metal giants, mesmerised. She had the Star in her hand, then she threw it straight at me. The Star came at me; once I saw it, I was hypnotised by it, until I realised it was heading straight for my face." "Seriously, how is that safe?" quizzed Nyrina, flummoxed.

Lemma ignored her and continued. "My scream sent all in the arena to the ground. As I ran away, the Star was chasing after me out of Mum's control. I dove under fences, jumped behind walls, trying to get away. Until I stopped and just stood still. Mum told me I screamed It's evil." A rather large smile adorns Lemma's face. "Evil, what was evil?" Nyrina sat mouth open wide, begging Lemma to continue.

"That was the point, Mother thought I meant the Star. I

didn't. I don't remember the next bit clearly. Apparently, I ran to a larger man as round as he was tall. Then I slid through his legs, clambered up his back, and hung from his neck, sinking my teeth into his left ear. I seemed to refuse to let go, like I was chewing on him. That's when mum said she knew what evil I saw. The man I had climbed on was filled with Rycor's taint."

"You sensed his evil before your mum?" Questioned Nyrina in her confusion. "Yep, I did, mum couldn't believe it, the Star flung itself at him, slicing over him in multiple directions until he collapsed to the ground. This is where I'm sure you will laugh. He fell backwards. There I was stuck under his shoulders and head, my legs kicking up and down one side of him, arms flailing on the other. I screamed, crying my eyes out as the Star hovered above my face, swaying like it watched me." Lemma chuckled as she spoke, especially watching the contorted facial expressions Nyrina made, her eyes enthralled by the story. "You got stuck under him, I'm sorry, Lemma, I can't help it, I'm sure you looked so cute," Nyrina said as she fell from her seat, curled up on the floor, hugging her knees, laughing.

"Ok, ok, I get it, little me pinned. It's a funny picture, but come on, stop now. Anyway… the Star hovered over me for a while until I fell asleep in the sand, exhausted from all the screaming. That's when it landed in my hand, and Mum said she felt the powers leave her. Yeah, so that's how I ended up as the next Queen and the holder of the Star. A screaming five-year-old pinned in place, asleep under a gargantuan man who bled from his left ear. Actually, I think he had a metal ear made to cover it after. I wonder if Mum would know?" Nyrina still couldn't get a hold of her laughter and did her best to apologise.

"Ok, we need to leave now, Ny, we have a thief to catch and a brothel to visit. Oh, and did I forget you're the bate?" Instantly, Nyrina stopped laughing. "I'm what?"

5

Settled At The Rising Sun

Khrom walked the cobbled road in the outer ring, looking for Lemma and Nyrina. Where are they? The princess said the sixth bell. "How's the wheat sacks?" came the shout. Khrom spun around, looking for who said it. Sure, it was the Princess. Did I imagine it? "Oi, Mud muncher over here." Spotting young ladies dressed in flowing dresses, their heads covered with scarves, as they walked towards him. Surely, it's not them.

"Couldn't tell it was us, could you? Gruladan won't know either then." Said Lemma with a strong determination in her voice, soon switching to a sarcastic one. "Don't you think Ny looks beautiful, Khrom?" Nyrina shuffled behind Lemma, trying to hide as best she could. Her face full of embarrassment, she whispered in Lemma's ear. "How could you? I already said I didn't want to lose the men's respect."

Khrom's jaw dropped open in utter disbelief as he spoke, "Nyrina! Is that truly you? You look stunning. Princess, why are you dressed this way anyway?" Lemma hushed him and whispered. "I'm not the princess at this moment, and Ny is the bait for Gruladan. I doubt any man will resist her; I can already tell you can't." Swiftly stepping back in shock, catching his heel on the edge of a cobble, Khrom fell, his face deep red and eyes pinned wide. "Erm, I…"

Lemma gave him no chance to speak. "Anyway, Khrom, on your feet! You're here as a guard. Once Ny or I get Gruladan from the Rising Sun, you'll be the one putting him in chains. When one of us says we are from Ashreb, you pounce. Clear? Oh, and as for your reward, you're now my second in command." Lemma just said it plainly, taking Khrom and Nyrina completely by surprise. "Thank you, my Princess, you do me the greatest of honours, and Ashreb as, in the town in the east?" Khrom replied. "Yes, Khrom, the town," Lemma said, looking at Nyrina, who just stood there in silence, still trying to hide from Khrom's view.

Walking down the cobblestone road at least twenty steps ahead of Khrom approaching the Rising sun, Lemma twirled and danced in every step pulling Nyrina with her showing both of them off to all onlookers, Nyrina garnering attention from all sides, whistles and cat calls filling the air, the occasional slap perforating the words as the wives and girlfriends of men silly enough to join in put them straight.

Lemma leaned in to the calls, responding with flirtatious looks and blowing kisses back at those who dared meet her eyes—increasing the volume of the half-cooked, slurred compliments of the men in the street.

The commotion had drawn many people from the inside of the Rising Sun, all excited to see what was happening. In the middle of the crowd stood the man they wanted, Gruladan. His only good eye locked on Lemma, not interested in Nyrina like all the others. *She looks more refined, a perfect flower to pick.* He thought.

Pushing through the crowd, Gruladan moved between Lemma and Nyrina, speaking as he puffed out his chest and used his most charismatic voice. "Why, what are two such fine young flowers doing heading to such a dang and dismal place such as the Rising Sun?" Lemma pretended to be caught in his words, faking a sweet and innocent smile whilst looking at her feet. "You see, kind sir, we are lost. We were told our new place of employment was around here." Lemma's words were sweet, but her thoughts were consumed by anger, the pain of Arrianna's bleeding and crying making her want to gut Gruladan where he stood. *I have you now. You one-eyed salt weasel, enjoy your last moments of freedom.* "I see, well, maybe you can drink

with me, and then I can personally guide you to where you seek."
Still, Gruladan acted suave and polite; his words fuelled Lemma's
anger more.

Nyrina, surprisingly, was playing her part very well,
considering the embarrassment she felt, twirling about, speaking to
the other men, slapping away hands as they tried to hold her, kicking
some in the shins to stifle their advances, to keep all the eyes on her.
Khrom could see what was happening, hanging back until Lemma
and Nyrina had the people enthralled and captivated, even though
his own thoughts betrayed a different set of feelings. *Nyrina, I
thought you were beautiful dressed in armour, but now you've sent my heart
fluttering. Will I ever be able to tell you?*

"Why, Sir, I've never been so gently spoken to by any man,
especially where we are from in Ashreb." Khrom heard his cue loud
and clear, pulling his sabre from his waist, and skilfully moving,
sticking at the building's edge and using the bystanders to remain
hidden. Nyrina still held them captive in her gaze until he was level
with Gruladan. From the building, he shoved outward, smashing two
men out of the way, sending them sideways. Not stopping, he was at
Gruladan's back, his sabre pressed against his throat. "You are mine
now, for the crime of thievery and drawing the blood of a royal. I
place you in my custody."

Gruladan tried to dip under the blade but was instantly
stopped by a swift and extremely forceful knee, careening straight

into his groin. An audible pop sent every man within hearing distance grasping at their own groin as he doubled over in agony, a wet red patch appearing and spreading on the outside of his trousers. "That was for Arrianna. The stocks are your punishment." Lemma said triumphantly.

Dragged from the Lower ring in cast iron chains, his groins still bleeding, Gruladan protested and wretched. Pulled into the centre ring by Khrom on grazed and bloodied knees, to the stocks sat under the city gallows. Shoved through a hole only just wide enough for his neck and wrists to fit in, A giant iron lock closed, pinning him in place. A notice was placed on the stand where he was being held.

"Stone as you wish, do not kill.

For twenty-one days, this man must remain here.

On his last day, should he not repent to Rysand for his crimes?

He will be tied to and fired from four of the wall ballistae."

6

Instant Noble

Lemma,

My dearest sister, you caused some chaos in the last few days. I'd almost forgotten the length you will go to for those you call friends and family. It lightens my heart to know that Auntie's Ring has been returned to Arrianna. I can only begin to imagine the relief she feels. That girl was dependent on Aunt to a fault. Sometimes, I wonder how she can even function. She would always be attached to Aunt, unable to be separated from her. So for that, I offer my sincerest thanks.

Anyway, sister, that is not why I write to you. I'm sure you are aware,

Mother dispatched me to Ashreb days ago, due to unseemly disturbances and strange goings-on. The local lord called for a royal visit, wishing for a royal presence among his people during their time of need. I have been here for three days at the time of writing. I suspect it will be around ten once you receive this letter, and many more before you can arrive. There are machinations beyond my scope afoot as just a mere Princess; I believe the issues lie inside the darker corners of people who wish our kingdom ill. I have been granted shelter in Lord and Lady Favener's home. Please join me there.

I beseech you, as the wielder of the Star, to come and help dig out the taint, as only you can.

With my love.

Faith

P.S. I can not wait to meet this new friend of yours. Nyrina was it? I hear she is quite beautiful and rivals even you.

Lemma sat in her chambers, preparing for another day of tedium and royal duties that she wished to avoid. On her little oak writing desk lay the letter from Faith, which still played in her mind. Under her breath, her words considered the request. "Faith, I will not have you stealing Ny. I know you, but all the same, this situation intrigues me." *Ny, sorry —erm —you may well be a perfect match for my sister's wit and desires.*

"Belladonna, would you be so Kind as to summon Ny for me? It looks as though we will be heading for Ashreb this day." Lemma asked one of the servant girls stationed in her room. *Just this once, I'll give the poor girl something to do, no matter what; she is here to aid me.* "At once, Princess." The words flowed over as Belladonna sped from the chamber out of the oak door in search of Nyrina.

****

"You called for me, Lemma" Nyrina's words pierced the silence of the room as she entered. "Why, Ny, have you become used to forgoing formality?" Lemma teased her, donning a large grin. "Oh, err, I'm sorry, my Prin." Lemma's laugh cut off Nyrina's words before she could finish the sentence. "Seriously, I get you every time. Will you ever learn?" "Lemma, why do you enjoy teasing me so?" "Because I can, Ny, because I can."

"Anyway, Ny, my sister Faith has requested us both in Ashreb. She has gotten in over her head, nothing unusual there, I suppose." Lemma chuckled, amused at her own words, before continuing to speak. "As a treat for us both, let us head to the master smith's. We need matching armour, just for this trip. "Lemma, I could never. The master smith is for nobility and above, far beyond my station." Stuttered Nyrina in a slowly forming panic.

"You believe your station too low, Ny. Seriously, you're my closest friend. Most of those brown nosing nobles would kill to be you." Lemmas' words came through strong and clear, causing Nyrina to panic further "Yes, I am aware, Lemma, especially of the scowls and shadowed words they speak of me." *You're not the one they deem too low-born to stand with you, do you not get that, Princess?* Lemma shook her head. "Oh, hush now, let them have their petty jealousy, I value the street cleaners over them anyway." "I can try." Nyrina's meek and unsure reply.

Into the city they walked, Nyrina doing as all expected, remaining a few steps behind Lemma as the people of Sciran greeted their princess. Every person smiled, bowed, and some even uttered words of praise and well-wishes. Lemma brushed it all aside, speaking with those who wished on equal footing, scolding those who presented with too much reverence for her position, reminding them that with her, it was unneeded.

As they finally approached the Master Smith's workshop, Nyrina let out an almost shockingly loud gasp, provoking yet more teasing from Lemma. "Yes, those hard straight stacks are some of the largest in the city, but you've seen plenty of stacked things already, haven't you, Nyrina? Khrom, for example." Nyrina ducked her head, tucking it into her chest, cheeks flushing pink with embarrassment. *Every mud-munching time, I really must learn not to open the door for her.*

In truth, the Master Smith's workshop was the grandest in all of Sciran, its looming chimneys almost as tall as the castle's towers, its sheer size nearly dwarfing the surrounding buildings by two, maybe three times their size. Simple enough where its oak doors set the centre of its frontage, welcoming anyone who entered. Like magic, they swung open all by themselves as Lemma and Nyrina approached.

"How? What? Who opened that door?" Nyrina spun on the spot, searching for anyone responsible. "Oh, Ny, it's one of the master's tricks. They open by themselves, and he still won't tell me how." An unusually quiet tone in Lemma's words as she smirked at Nyrina's discombobulation.

"Princess, welcome. To what do I owe this pleasure?" Questioned the master smith, words muffled below his ample beard. "You still look the same as you did ten years ago, Smith. How do you still look as ancient as the city, yet your eyes are forever young?" A certain level of cheek permeated the air among Lemma's words. "It's all in the work, Princess, it ages the body but not the mind." The smith swiftly replied. "To the business at hand, Princess, how may I serve you today?"

Those words seemed to light a fire under Lemma. Her energy and movements were animated and comical as she tried to explain the style and colours she wished for within the armour she planned for her and Nyrina to share. "So, Princess, from your word, I gather you want a set for you and the young lady with you, silver with blue tones, leather under amour as always. For you, a clasp to hold the Star and for your friend a sheath to match it, upon the chest." The smith's words were abruptly interrupted. "Shh! That's a surprise for Ny."

All this time, Nyrina had been lost in the wonder of the workshop, unable to fix her gaze to one single spot, trying to absorb every minuscule detail. *Who knows if I'll ever see these hallowed halls again? I must remember them.* Her thoughts contained her until she heard her name, snapping her back to reality. "Yes, Lemma, you called?" asked Nyrina, bewildered. "Ny, one day you will get used to it, I'm sure," Lemma said, smiling and shaking her head slightly.

"This way," called the Smith, throwing out his arm to indicate the door on the opposite side of the room, and waited for Lemma and Nyrina to enter the room beyond. "Ny, you're first, hop on that little podium and watch the smith work." *You're in for a treat; it still hypnotises me watching him work.* Stepping up onto the podium, Nyrina waited as the smith moved around her in circles, examining each part of her body, causing her to break into an anxious thought. *This is not fun, Lemma. All he does is stare.*

A sudden click of the Smiths' fingers, and Nyrina's clothes vanished into thin air. In the same instant, a full suit of supple, lightly tanned leather encased her entire body, hugging every curve. A squeal shocked the room. "What? How? Ooh, this is comfy, I can move so freely." The realisation in Nyrina's voice had Lemma in stitches, as she watched. Another clap of the Smith's hand and Metal boots of trident silver metal appeared on Nyrina's feet, followed by interconnecting plates of trident armour running the length of her legs.

The Smith paused, furrowing his brow, clearly unhappy with something. He stepped forward and hovered his hands over Nyrina's legs. Tracing the outside of the armour, the colour began to change, a steady gradient of Scirainian blue mixing into the silver. Content that the colour was right, he stepped back.

Another click of his fingers and a plate armour top in the same colour appeared, tailored to each movement of Nyrina's body. It covered her hips to chest, where it swiftly transitioned to a delicate chain mesh halter-style top that came together in a delicate circular choker around her throat, allowing her skin to breathe freely.

Silently, Nyrina stood, her eyes widening, her mouth agape, as her mind was filled with wonder and awe. *This armour is too much, but it feels so right on me. Even though it showcases my body, I feel safe and secure, as if I can show the world the real me.*

Lemma danced about, feeling the rhythm of the euphoria all around her, swept up in the excitement of the moment. "Ny, by all that is holy, I cannot express how amazing this armour looks on you and how stunning you are." "Lemma, please, it will be nothing compared to you, but I admit it feels amazing." Nyrina's words echoed with pride.

The smith still hadn't finished. Again, his hand hovered over Nyrina, moving along the rear of the upper plate, lettering materialising as he passed. Lemma read them aloud. "First Commander Nyrina Tyrell. Princess Royal Guard." Unsure of the words she heard, Nyrina spoke, "What did you just say?"

Lemma stepped to the front of Nyrina, a solid regal look upon her face and the Star of Sciran in hand. "Kneel, Nyrina Tyrell, before your future Queen." Shock grabbed Nyrina's very soul. *What is happening here? Lemma, what are you doing?* It felt to Nyrina in that moment as if an unknown force overwhelmed her very being, pushing down from above, shoving her to one knee.

"Nyrina Tyrell, in recognition of your service to the crown and your aid to me, Princess Royal Lemma Sciranton." Pausing to place the Star flat against Nyrina's forehead, then speaking again. "You are hereby granted the title of First Commander of the Princess Royal Guard, and all title and land henceforth associated with this station."

Nyrina buckled under her own weight, collapsing to the floor in a heap at Lemma's words, tears flooding her face, and rolling down her cheeks. Sobbed words met Lemma's ears. "But I don't deserve such height, I have only performed my duty as a soldier of the realm, any would have done the same as I. My princess, I will guard you with my life." Star clipped back to her waist, Lemma forgot all formality and dived at Nyrina, hugging her tight. "Ny, you deserve it, and besides, in that armour, just looking at you will stop any man dead."

Grunting from behind them, the smith interrupted. "Princess, I haven't done yours. Will you please take the podium?" Lemma helped Nyrina to stand and replaced her on the podium, watching and waiting for her armour to appear. It did in the same colour as Nyrina's, almost matching in every detail except one: the crest of Sciran etched into the trident, in solid Scirainian blue.

One last item brought to the room by the apprentice from the silk masters' shop, two green-rimmed purple cloaks with attached hoods, was presented to both of them and then placed over Lemma's and Nyrina's shoulders and clipped into place.

7

Ashreb

Four days had passed while Lemma and Nyrina rode and camped on repeat, just the burning sun over them—the green Scirainian Plains under their horses' hooves. Lemma had become increasingly aware of a strangeness overhead. Each day, she observed the slightest shift in the sun's position, as it moved from the east back to the north. Every day, it had set just a little more northward than it should. As the first outlying buildings of Ashreb came into view, Lemma began to think. *I know I'm not seeing things, but Ny hasn't seemed to notice anything. It's genuinely odd.*

"We are nearly there, Lemma, a few more minutes. Where

did Princess Faith say she stayed?" Receiving no response, Nyrina poked at Lemma's side from her steed. "Huh, what did you say? Sorry, my mind was elsewhere." "We are about to arrive. Where do we need to meet Princess Faith?" Nyrina repeated. "Oh, the Lord's home, Faith should be there with him and his wife."

****

Dropping from their saddles at the main gate of Lord Favener's Manor house, a grandiose structure in comparison, built from local yellow sandstone mined from the Drake mountains that lay slightly further east than Ashreb. Clear glazed windows spread from end to end. *What in Sciran? If each window is a room, they must have twenty windows on the bottom floor alone; only the castle has more.* Nyrina's mind struggled to absorb it. "Oh, quite the building. I've seen better back home." Lemma joked.

From the red-painted door, the call came. "Sister, you're here." "Faith, you knew I was coming. Why are you so surprised?" Lemma's reply came across as somewhat angsty and irritated. "Oh, and who is this fine friend with you? Her Beauty certainly rivals yours, Lemma." Nyrina blushed wordlessly. *Usually, I'd go shy, but I liked it. Why?* "For all that's holy, Faith! You could have at least invited us in before the flirting began." Lemma scolded before introducing Nyrina, with an all too-knowing smile. Faith turned on her heels, outstretched arms extending to the red door of the manor. "This way, if you will, ladies."

Nyrina shuffled her leather boots as she edged past Princess Faith, trying to avoid eye contact with her. *Please let me inside. I don't want to blush more in your presence, Princess.* Lemma strode confidently past Faith, heading for the door. Lord Favener appeared with a smile beaming on his face as he dropped into a low bow, welcoming her.

In the hall, the ladies gathered. Lord Favener joined them, followed by a small contingent of maids carrying a selection of elegantly presented snacks. "Your highnesses and M'lady, I bid you welcome. Unfortunately, I can only offer this meagre spread at this time. Tonight, a grand meal for the town is arranged with you as the special guests." Lemma shot a glare over the distance between her and Faith. *You didn't stop the formalities, by Rysand, sister, will you never stop trying to make me act like you?*

Nyrina's nostrils were drawn to the sweet scents, which led her to the nearest maid. "Young Lady, what are these small pinkish curled grub things?" "M'lady, they are freshwater artisanal Shrimp, they taste of nectar, a local delicacy." Undetermined and common, Nyrina grabbed a handful from the silver platter, placing the first Shrimp to her lip, tasting it. *They taste like I'm eating the freshest honey.* Her mind betrayed her, as her words spilt forth. "Lemma, Lemma, they taste like I can't explain it, it's like the freshest honey, but at the same time, air ." Lemma looked on, laughing wholeheartedly, listening to her and Faith's objections. "Lemma, she calls you by name, not title!?" Lemma interrupted, "Faith, do be quiet, I told her to." Switching to a whisper, then saying. "Maybe she will call you more than Faith or princess if you treat her right." Faith stood stunned in silence. Nyrina recognised Lemma's cheeky grin straight away. *Lemma, what did you set me up for now?*

****

Morning birds sang outside the manor's window as Lemma woke, snuggled inside the satin sheet on top of the feather mattress, groaning about being awake so early. "Grrr! Birds, go mud munch somewhere else. I need to sleep." Dry-eyed, she dragged herself up to her feet and headed to the door, though she could already hear Faith. *Still a morning person, you never change.*

Breakfast was served in the dining hall. The smell of freshly fried Mullock spreading throughout the manor—toasted bread fresh from the kitchen oven, tempting all residents to take up a seat. Lemma sat, still waking up, enjoying her food as Faith brought the table's conversation around to all business. "Lemma, my dearest sister, I told you a strange thing occurred here. It has worsened over the last few days; since I arrived, one person has disappeared every week. Now we've had three in two days." Lady Favener joined the conversation. "Your majesty, the only clue was the dragging marks of blood. We found nothing else."

Lemma shook her head, disappointed "So what you're telling me is that you actually know nothing, I'll have to look myself." *If anything, it sounds like an animal attack, though the amount is concerning.* Finishing up breakfast, Lemma left the table, signalling for Nyrina to follow, and then asked Faith. "Where did the attacks happen?" "Last one was behind the Mazie Hay Inn," shouted Lady Favener as Faith failed to answer.

Following the windy mud lane, Lemma and Nyrina came to the Maizy Hay, searching the front area; no marks or indications of an attack could be found. "Perhaps since it happens from the shadows, we should check the back of the building, Lemma," Nyrina suggested whilst moving around the side of the building. The corner of her eye caught a glimpse of something dug into the wooden upright strut; she looked closer. *What is that?* Inside a scrappy, splintered hole, she found a black claw, the very sharp end of one.

"Lemma, I've got something here, I think it's a claw." Lemma ran over, taking the claw from Nyrina's hand, looking at it intensely. *If it weren't black, I'd say it's a plains Kitsune, their claws are blue.* "Nyrina, have you ever seen a plains Kitsune?" "No, I've heard of them but never seen them. They are placid creatures by the tales." Lemma nodded in agreement. "I've only ever seen one, and that was with a travelling merchant, when I was a child, but I'll never forget the claw; it gave several guards scars."

That was the final clue to be found in daylight hours. So they waited. As the final rays of light dipped from view, the clear, black sky lit up like a blanket of pinhole lights. Hidden, waiting on the front deck of the Mazie Hay, they sat behind stacked beer barrels. The sound of scraping and scratching clung to the building, irritating their ears like an itch they couldn't scratch. From inside the inn, the final patron walked out, turning down the side of the inn. Silence. His steps gone, his drunken song missing. Lemma and Nyrina leapt the guard rail to the ground at the inn's corner.

Nyrina saw the Star light up like a hundred candles at Lemma's waist. "Lemma what on Apprite, the Star." Lemma pulled the Star from its clasp. Nyrina unsheathed her straight sword, plunging into the darkness. The stars in the sky lit their way, and as they saw the trail of blood on the ground, they began the hunt.

The trail of blood led them behind the inn, through the building's alleyways and toward Lord Favener's home. Crawling up to the manor's garden wall, a long, thin line of wet, blood-soaked soil still guided them further around the manor. Eventually, they stopped at the rear, facing the open plains. "Where did it go?" Lemma asked the air. *The Star still reacts; it's near.*

Walking out into the open, into the longer grass several meters past the rear wall, the Star glowed stronger. "Ny, it's close, I feel it. Ny?" Lemma looked to her left and then to her right. Nyrina had disappeared. "Lemma, I'm over here", Nyrina shouted fearfully from somewhere in front. "Keep calling, I'll follow your voice," Lemma shouted out. Careful in her stride, Lemma carried on into the grass, ever growing, soon standing at her shoulder height.

Stopping to listen again and calling out for Nyrina, Lemma realised she was close to Nyrina's voice, which seemed almost at her feet. Her right hand pushed the tall, thick stalks of grass aside. She saw Nyrina waist-deep in the ground. "I think I found it, a burrow maybe?" Lemma's face betrayed her before the laughter left her mouth, a pure smirk running ear to ear. "I think you have, now let's get you out."

Gripping Nyrina's wrists firmly, Lemma pulled with all her might, struggling, Nyrina's body not moving, like the ground gripped at her waist, sucking her further in. Nyrina began screaming blue murder. "Something has my ankle! Pull harder." Planting her feet shoulder-width apart and leaning back, pulling as hard as she could, Lemma fell tumbling backwards, as Nyrina's scream ripped through the silent night air, accompanied by a sudden pop. "My Arm is limp, I can't move it." Lemma looked back at her friend; surely enough, her arm hung swaying with every slight movement, clearly not connected to its joint anymore.

From the hole came the growls and guttural screams of a man being torn apart, then the loudest Silence, followed by a rasp, the final breath of his life extinguished.

In the next moment, a black form emerged, crawling up slowly, aided by the shadows. A Kitsune, its flesh rotten and fur-less, three of its four tails reduced to stubs of protruding bone. Its eyes, the reddest of red, stared straight at them, each paw ending in jet black claws covered in the blood of its previous victims.

"Nyrina, make for the town, you can't fight like that," Lemma ordered. "I will not leave your side, my honour and posting will not allow it." Nyrina gathered her sword in her good hand, holding it out. Lemma stood, Star held between her sprawled fingers around its centre. The Kitsune moved with speed, unlike any Lemma had ever seen before, pouncing high, steps away from her, claws outstretched, already swiping as it descended. Lemma used the last second to back-flip away. Her armour boot colliding with the Kitsune's paw, sending its body spinning, twirling to the floor, where it landed on its side, howling from the shock.

Nyrina, using her only good arm, thrust forward the tip of her blade, glancing off the severed bone where the tail used to be. The strike served its purpose to distract the Kitsune's attention just long enough for Lemma to launch the Star. Horizontally, it skimmed the floor, ripping through the two left-hand legs, cutting free the paws in a flurry of anguished screams, for them to fly into the darkness—black, viscous blood pouring from the stubbed end of each leg. Quick flashes of blue lightning lashed out at the ground, causing it to erupt upward and raise a thick cloud of dust.

On stub and paw, the Kitsune came again, unable to jump and plunging its blood-stained fangs straight for Nyrina's legs. From within the settling dust, the Star returned vertical in its spin. It slashed deep into the gut of the Kitsune, lifting it clean into the air and carrying it forward. A lightning bolt collided with its front right leg, removing it from the centre mass.

The Kitsune fell back to the ground, and the Star returned to Lemma's hand. Nyrina, frozen in fear, her pupils fixed behind the Kitsune. A moment of clarity made her call. "Lemma, the Kitsune's shadow, destroy it. It acts like a rope, stretching and moving with it." The Star tore the ground, cutting a straight line from Lemma to the tether, like a pinwheel slicing it and spinning in place. The lightning struck the same spot, gauging the shadow and cutting its connection.

In utter pain and rage, the Kitsune howled as the shadow receded from it. Nyrina was able to break from her fear, bolting for its head. The full length of her blade stabbed precisely through its eye, piercing the brain beyond. A final guttural howl sounded from the Kitsune, reverberating in the air itself, then it fell dead, pulling Nyrina with it. She tumbled, unable to stop the fall, her chest crashed into the Kitsune's lifeless body, a scream forced from her throat as the spiny bone of the Kitsune's tail tore into her side.

Speeding to Nyrina's side, lifting her. "Ny, are you ok?" Meekly, Nyrina spoke. "Cuts and bruises, cuts and bruises, what about you?" blood soaked from the inside of Nyrina's armour spreading throughout the leather as they both struggled walking back to the manor, exhausted and battered.

From the manor, they ran all the staff, Lord and Lady,

princess and pauper. Gathering Nyrina from Lemma, they placed her upon a hastily constructed stretcher. Rushing Nyrina inside, Faith came beside her, scrambling to undo armour straps, and pulling them piece by piece from her body. The pained cries, coursing from deep in Nyrina's throat as she did, were utterly ignored.

Faith pulled a loose sheet from the base of the bed, forcing her hand inside the open wound, stemming the blood flow. Faith screamed, "Nyrina, I will save you. Maid, fetch me a needle and thread quickly." Snatching the needle from the maid, stabbing the razor-sharp point through Nyrina's skin. She lost her grip as Nyrina bucked upwards, screaming. "Anyone hold her down?" Faith called out for aid. A maid and Lord Favener grabbed Nyrina's body, pinning her down.

Held still, Faith successfully stitched the wound, sealing it shut, assessing Nyrina's shoulder next. She examined it, limp, hanging over the side of the bed. "Nyrina, bite down on the sheets. This will hurt worse than walking through fire." In a coruscation, Faith held Nyrina's arm as she snapped it upward and inward, forcing the joint back into place. Nyrina screamed, "You mud-munching salt weasel!" Before passing out in bed.

A chair was placed at Nyrina's bedside, where Faith sat, applying cold towels regularly throughout the night. She caressed her arm and whispered. "Nyrina, please wake. You have captured my admiration. I want to speak with you." Lemma stood at the chamber door listening. *Faith, I knew you liked her; you do this for no one… ever.*

8

I Must Travel Alone

Nyrina finally opened her eyes in the early hours. Her body still aching, the section of her side that Faith had stitched burned. *I swear I can feel it healing, knitting together. This is not going to be fun*; she rolled onto her left-hand side, putting her back to the wall to see a full view of the room. Princess Faith still sat on the ridged Wooden chair. Ok, I'm pretty sure I'm not the princess here. How does this keep happening? Now two of them look after me.

Nyrina noticed a pool of lightly tinted, red water as she observed Faith slumped over, her head down, her chin on her chest. A wet towel remained in her hand and hung towards the floor at her side. By Rysand, if I keep my new rank after this escapade, it will be by the skin of my teeth. What Nyrina didn't know was that Faith had already spoken with Lemma regarding the situation and her concerns over Nyrina's continued journey.

Lemma lay on her wooden double bed, her head resting on the cream, fine fur pillows atop the satin sheets of the same colour. Not enjoying knowing that Nyrina's was the complete opposite of her grand bedroom that the lord had provided. The night had plagued her, preventing any dream; seeing her friend injured left the foulest taste of guilt in her throat; nothing she had done had shifted it. Drinking, gargling, forced coughing, and even going as far as to try the use of a small brush to clear it. That idea failed miserably, inducing her to vomit, which coincidentally didn't help either.

Now, thanks to the fight, she hadn't slept at all. Well, maybe in dribs and drabs here and there when her eyes became too heavy, but the vision of Nyrina soon forced them open again. *I need to apologise; I need to see that she's okay. Most of all, leave her in Faith's care.* Pushing up on her arms and twisting round, she extricated her body from the bed, moving to the room's dark wooden dresser, full-length mirror and gown stand, taking the Scirainian blue and purple gown that Lady Favener had placed there for her use. Wrapping up in the gown, spotting a pair of purple fluffy mule-style slippers under the front edge of the dresser. *Save's wearing my boots, I suppose, but why can't they be regular slippers?*

Fully covered in clothes she would rather not wear, Lemma left the room. *God, I look like a pampered princess. I look like Faith on a typical day.* Sauntering down the well-lit corridor, observing the multiple portraits of man, woman and child hanging about the vermilion wall tucked between the numerous windows. *This Lord, if I didn't know better, after meeting him, shows himself as a right pompous salt weasel. The amount of grand art and expensive pieces I've seen says he doesn't care for the people, but his actions say otherwise.* Stopping, looking up at one particular picture, a familiar scene to anyone who lived in Sciran but strangely different to any Lemma had seen before.

Speculation moved across Lemma's face as her emerald green eyes danced over the all too familiar scene of the first keeper of the Star. There was something in the picture that was not the same as the multitude she had seen before in the background, just on the very edge of the frame. A blackened sword with veins of red running the length, and flames dancing along it. *That sword's image stirs something in me. Oh, whatever, never mind, I'll ask Lord Favener about it later.*

The stairs to the ground floor sprawled out and downward, their twirling structure almost had Lemma dizzy as she peered over the bannister. *Glad the castle doesn't have these.* As she descended, she heard the hustle and bustle of the house staff preparing breakfast this morning. Passing the kitchen doorway, the smell of fresh fried vegetables and an unfamiliar meat pleasantly drifted past Lemma's nose. On she walked to the room where Nyrina slept, determined to diminish her own fears and those of her best friend.

Nyrina still lay, Staring Deeply at the sleeping Princess Faith, her eyes moving over her body as she admired her form. *She looks so much like Lemma, yet her features are much fairer and daintier; they have not seen the evils of battle.* Nyrina's blood rushed from her face in shock, her heart began to beat faster and raced harder the more she stared. *What is this feeling? I want to know her. Her very scent invigorates me. By Rysand, I like, like her, no, no, it can't be possible? Can it? Maybe it's gratitude for her care. No, wait, I fluttered the first time I saw her. Aah, what do I do?*

The door reverberated under the strength of Lemma's knock as she waited impatiently to be invited in. "Enter," Nyrina called, startling Faith awake and out of her chair to the floor. Faith's head bounced off the chair's seat before landing in Nyrina's lap. "Princess, are you ok?" Nyrina called as she tried to move in the bed, her stitches stretching, two tearing, and the wound around them reopening. "Ny, you utter mud muncher, you're too injured to move like that. Stay still. Faith, will you get off the floor?" Lemma scolded them both as she entered the room, seeing the shenanigans within.

Faith rushed to the table, grabbed the needle and thread, and went back to the bed. "Nyrina, stay still. I need to reseal the wound. Lemma…" Faith's words were cut short when she saw what Lemma was wearing. *It's like looking in a mirror. Why the hell is Lemma wearing something like that? Oh, what a position Princess Faith ended up in. What does Lemma think happened?*

Stitching finished, Faith sat back down and faced Lemma, laughing her head off. "See, Lemma, I was always right, you look as good in a robe as you do in armour, a right pretty princess." "Shut it, Faith, I do not!" Lemma retorted with an angry outburst, her eyebrows dipping as she scowled at both of them. Nyrina still just lay there, chuckling at Lemma's outfit, *Mullock's dung, laughing hurts, but I can't stop.* Continuing to think, *Rysand, you can tell they're sisters.* Lemma stepped further into the room, a strong and visible purpose in each step, the room's whole ambience dropping slowly, cooling the only way it could be described.

"Ny, you are not going to be fit for travel any time soon, I can see that. Faith, you've still got the citizens to calm and soothe. That's why I'm going to travel further afield alone, the darkness here isn't the first I've faced or even felt." Lemma's words hurt Nyrina, but she understood the sense behind them, just as Faith did, and chose to remain silent, unlike Faith. "Sister, you want to leave already? What about Nyrina's care?" This, Nyrina decided to answer. "I just need rest. Princess Faith, Lemma doesn't need me for this; My presence would hinder her journey. If I do need help, the Lord and Lady, I'm sure, will aid me. Do you not think your highness!?"

Faith fled the room in silence, unhappy that her sister's demands had overruled her, but one thought still lingered. *I will have*

Nyrina to myself. Lemma took the seat next to Nyrina's bed, speaking with a smile. "Ny, don't worry, Faith is like that all the time, hates to lose. Besides, it will do you good to rest and befriend her." "Ok Lemma, but please be safe." Nyrina's words, although spoken quickly, held a lot of emotion: shyness, embarrassment, and joy, all mixed on her face. *I wish you well, princess. Return soon.* Nyrina lay back down after the brief burst of activity, which drained her enough to sleep again.

Lemma left her to sleep, heading off to the kitchen, hoping to catch even the latter end of those delicious smells from before and hopefully get to eat some of it too. In the kitchen sat the Lord and Lady Favener, casually talking between themselves over a breakfast of pan-fried vegetables and meat. Seeing Lemma enter, they immediately stood, bowing and offering her a place at the head of the table. "Sit please, I don't need the formality, treat me as you would a normal person. Now, what's for breakfast? Those smells intrigue me, and my taste buds salivate." Sitting where the Lord and Lady had shown her, Lemma took a plate, grabbed the serving tongues and began filling her own plate, much to the amazement of all around. *Please stop looking at me, I want to eat,* she thought as she spotted all the eyes on her.

"Lord Favener, I saw a portrait of Sciran on my way down this morning. It seemed different from most others I've seen. A random sword appeared to be in full swing behind her. Do you know what that sword is?" Lemma asked with a quizzical tone in her voice as she moved to take a large piece of meat. "Actually, your highness, that portrait was one of my great-great-great-grandfather's, about five or six great-grandfathers ago. He had heard the tale of the Rysender, the three weapons forged by Rysand and humans at the time of the creation wars, thousands of years ago. I'm sure you know it's the reason the Gorge split the continent and such. We all know the Star of Sciran is one of them, and that another took the Echidna flame on the death of Hagen, the first king of Occard. The third weapon was lost."

Lemma sat nodding, listening and chewing on a rather fatty piece of meat, occasionally saying yes between bites, as she bid Lord Favener to continue his tale. "So when he painted it, he had the sword added as a reminder that more than one existed, honestly, I know nothing further, oh, except one thing that the weapons are all connected, family or kin to each other, and when needed, they will find each other again, or so I was told."

Lemma considered the words the Lord spoke, words that the Book of Sciran echoed the sentiment of, the one book she had read countless times since receiving the Star, a comprehensive history of the country she would one day rule, started by Sciran herself to teach each new generation. "Thank you, Lord Favener, I thought as much, though it's nice to have things confirmed." A loud, rushed knock began at the main door of the Manor, bringing everyone's attention to it. A valet opened the door and stood at the entrance, a sweaty, exhausted young man in a messenger uniform. "I bring a letter for her Highness, Princess Lemma, of much importance, if she is here." He asked in panted breaths.

Lemma sprang from her seat and sprinted from the kitchen, headed for the door, hearing the panic within the messenger boy's voice. *Only something of great importance would see a messenger sent here for me.* Snatching the folded paper from the messenger, seeing her mother's queen's seal pressed into the red wax crossing the join, she ripped it open, reading it.

My dearest daughter,

A great darkness has begun to stalk our plains. Not only did you go to see this with your own eyes, but it was also at your sister's request. I believe you sensed it before you left. I now bring even graver news received from Kymei point on our southeastern border, amongst the Drake mountains. Reports have been received of a creature haunting the small hamlets, forcing their complete evacuation to Dracklow fort, some five days' walk west of it. The reports have described it as neither man nor beast but something in between, sinister and dark. I fear it may be one of the evil god Rycor's minions; as such, the only person capable of dispatching it without the need for others is you. If it weren't for the description, I wouldn't ask this of you; instead, I would send the army. Please investigate and, if necessary, eliminate the creature forthwith.

Any further reports or concerns will be sent to you there. I am horrified to think that evil may be returning even in the smallest of ways.

With love and care,
Your Mother,
Queen Catherine of Sciran

The shock of the letter shook Lemma to the very core. Upon finishing, she dropped it, leaving it to float slowly to the floor, while she screamed to all that could hear her. "Fetch me Several Days of food and water, see my horse loaded and my tent stowed ready, I must leave immediately for the southeast."

9

To Kymei Point

Flying from the town aboard her freshly loaded Scirainian Mare, its jet-black fur sleek and well-groomed, its mane short and well-kept, Lemma sat in a supple and cushioned Brown leather saddle. She flicked the reins against the horse's neck, urging it onward, with a swift tap to its hindquarters to reinforce the necessity for speed. Ashreb soon disappeared into the rear horizon, and the Plains of Sciran spread out wider than the eye could see. In front of Lemma, nothing but the green grass and the sporadic patches of wild flowers. I face five days of non-stop riding until Kymei, with no breaks except for sleep.

The first three days of riding were unhindered, Easy nights' camping under the stars, and plentiful, easily collected wood and dry grass at each location. Every stop helped keep the travelling rations from being eaten, and she chose locations based on the readily available wild edible plants. Plucking the curly craddocks from the firm soil was quite the task for Lemma. Her fingers still ached, her nails still held the dirt under them. *Digging those Craddocks was worth it; they are delicious, especially the wild ones, which are just sweeter. I'm not looking forward to the dried meat and stone-hard bread tonight.*

The days spent in the saddle, just riding the plains, had begun to leave their mark. Lemma's behind had started to redden; the friction between the leather of her pants and that of the saddle rubbed her in all the wrong ways. At some points, it felt like she sat in a fire, with the only solace she had found being to soak a hessian sack in water, then placing it underneath her rear end. *If this continues, I'll end up walking.* Her mind focused on the nagging pain building again beneath her. The pain distracted her enough to prevent her eyes from locking onto the group of people who approached her on foot. From ahead, the people yelled, trying to garner Lemma's attention unsuccessfully.

As Lemma's steed came upon the group, tearing full speed, a small child let out a high-pitched screech, scaring the horse. Bucking up on its rear legs, throwing Lemma from the saddle, into the air, she flew, letting loose a Scream of her own just before colliding with the ground, smashing down hard on her back, bouncing and coming to rest, stunned in disbelief. An older gentleman from the group had gathered the flailing reins of the horse, calming it, while two of the group's ladies ran to Lemma, lying flat on her back. Lemma lay there, mind in turmoil, several questions flying through it. *What on Apprite happened? What made the horse throw me? Great, my shoulder is in agony now, I suppose at least I can't feel the pain in my ass.*

"Lady? Lady, are you ok?" The younger of the two ladies exclaimed, coming to Lemma's side and looking down at her. The girl peered down, observing Lemma's eyes open and alert, and breathed a sigh of relief. "Can you hear me? Are you hurt?" the girl asked again, much calmer and more collected. Lemma stared up at the girl, almost sure she could see several tiny Stars of Sciran spinning in front of her. Lemma pulled her thoughts together and spoke, "Erm… I think I'm ok, my shoulder is banged up, but I'll be fine. What happened?" Taking the outstretched young lady's hand, Lemma came to her feet, aided. Standing, she felt the pain in her right shoulder. *Nothing feels out of place, just a knock, I hope.*

"I'm Lemma. I apologise for this. Who are you people?" The two ladies parted, stepping in opposite directions as the older man led the horse back to Lemma's side as he spoke. "We are travellers from Occard, we have fled the rule of Quinten. I'm Harrod, the family head." Lemma stared at them, considering the options that she currently had. *They are refugees from an enemy nation. I can't leave them, but I can't take them with me. What do I do here?* Humble words left Lemma's lips, "Harrod, your luck may be about to change. Do you carry anything I may write with?" Harrod looked perplexed as he called to the other companions. "Someone bring me parchment and a quill if we have them?"

A younger gentleman pulled a scrap of Parchment from his pack. Meanwhile, a young lady managed to find a charcoal pencil in hers, but no one could discover ink or a quill. Taking the parchment and charcoal from them both, Lemma leaned against the saddle of her horse and began to write.

Dearest Sister and Ny,

I met this group of Occardian refugees travelling to Kymei at mother's request. Please, see them taken in and housed in Ashreb. Let them amalgamate with the locals if needed, and aid them in finding work. I don't know if they have any skills; you will need to assess that for yourselves. Ny, I hope your side and shoulder heal well and that my sister treats you well. I hope to return soon, but mother has said in her correspondence that there may be more for me to do.

Sincerely,

Princess Royal,
Lemma.

On handing the letter to Harrod, she explained. "This Letter will guarantee your safety in the town of Ashreb. Ask for Nyrina or Princess Faith on your arrival and give them the note. I can do no more at this time." Taking the letter in hand, Harrod looked at the words on the parchment. *What? She is the princess royal.* "All of you kneel." He screamed to the group. "We are in the presence of the Princess Royal; she has granted us aid and a hope for a new home." Each of the family members took to their knees, bowing and thanking Lemma profusely. A cold look crossed Lemma's face "Get up, all of you. I don't ask my own people to kneel or bow. I certainly do not expect it of you."

The group stood, all wondering what to do for the best. "But Your Highness, we need to bow; is it not a crime?" Harrod probed unease in each word. Lemma shook her head and answered him. "In Occard, maybe, and to any other Scirainian royal, but not me, I serve the people, not the other way round." "Then you have our thanks, Princess. Can I please ask the way in which we now need to head?" "Of course, Harrod, did you observe the direction I rode from? That has taken me three days nonstop on horseback. So, probably five days at walking pace." Lemma gave the instruction clearly and saw the family on their way before jumping back into the saddle and heading off.

The night and the next day passed without incident; Lemma's

shoulder quickly healed and became painless. Unfortunately, this meant she could once again feel the chafe of the saddle against her backside. In the distance, the first wooden hut of Kymei point had tipped the horizon. Lifting her head skyward to the top of the peak behind it, there stood the tall and grand stone tower that surveyed the lands beyond. *I wonder what it's like over in the Arathy plains? I've only ever visited its capital once before, so maybe one day I should travel there.* Slowing the horse to a walk as she entered Kymei, Lemma felt the chill; she could have sworn her bones froze over. It was the type of chill only an empty vestige of civilisation could cause. It felt so wrong that every house in the hamlet, even the small trading stand, just stood empty. It looked like people had just disappeared, chimneys still smoked, the livestock still wandered about aimlessly, unattended. *What does this mean for the tower? Have the soldiers been evacuated as well?*

Hopping down from the horse's back and leading it to the hitching post outside what looked like a tiny guest house, Lemma tied the horse up, leaving it there to graze the hay left in the feeder. She walked up the guest house steps, pressing firmly on the entrance door, feeling it give under the pressure of her hands and swing open. Inside, nothing of any real note, just a small stand with the log book sat on top, a quill placed in the ink well to its left. Calling out to receive no reply. "Hello, is anyone there?" *It's truly empty, I'll use the bed and leave the payment.*

10

Tormented Tower

Leaving the empty guesthouse at first light, Lemma stumbled back through the open door aghast at the sight in the road. Her horse was dead. Its head still hung from the reins at the post, its body torn to pieces, intestines and lungs pulled through the gaping hole in its stomach. The ground was a matted brown mess of red blood. Across the road, two of its legs cast high up on the roof of the opposite building, the other two on the deck in front of the guest house. "In all the benevolence, what could have done this!?" Lemma screamed into the open air.

Lemma ran to the horse, the Severed head cradled in her arms, as she looked into its dormant eyes. Lemma cried silently as her mind flooded with memories of the years she had spent riding in the saddle alongside her mount. A silent ache filled her body, racked with guilt. As a quiet fury filled the air, she contemplated what caused it. Only a creature full of taint, a creature so vile. Lemma forced her eyes from the grotesque sight she held in her hands out into the street, tracking the Blood that smeared its way along the road to the base of the mountain. Lemma came to a stop as the rough, muddy road gave way to the rocky steps leading to the tower.

Finally able to process the scene, Lemma gathered up any remaining items that were within sight of the horse's severed head and placed them on the deck. *They will be safe here till I return.* Making sure to avoid the blood-soaked area, she jogged towards the mountain's path, determined to conquer the height of that foreboding tower and any foul beast within. *This is my country, and I will protect it,* her only thoughts. The first step onto the rocky path, a coarse and dishevelled mess of rock carved into steps, each one becoming increasingly flatter and more defined as she moved up the mountainside. Turning back to check the distance she had walked, Lemma was impressed by the fact that it seemed to be more than halfway, which spurred her onward.

Fatigue had begun to set in by the midday sun, forcing Lemma to rest. Finding a flat rock on which to sit, she untied the water sack at her waist and drank, slowly in big gulps, between laboured breaths. *Not too much further now, and...* Lemma's thought got cut short, a deafening screech drove the serene silence away from her ears, piercing into her very self. *I sense the taint of Rycore; it fills the very air about me. It's stronger than I've ever felt before.* Struck by the fear that this level of taint caused her, Lemma imagined a beast that must be several times her own size, at least twice as strong and fed by the very shadows themselves.

Speaking with herself out loud, "Move forward, you must, the Star will protect you, and so will Rysand. No one else can do this." From the rock, she lifted herself back to her feet, pushing ever upwards, step by step, moment by moment, as she drew closer to the tower and that tormented soul she would need to face.

The final step seemed to dwarf the others; Lemma's perception of size seemed off. *How can one step be so different to all the others?* Lemma felt as though her eyes were deceiving her. The star sat dimly glowing at her hip, sensing something ominous. This step would require climbing, not in the same way you step up a single step, but like she would need to pull herself up and over a cliff's edge. *I've been to places that seem like they warp time, but never the objects around me.* Latching on with both hands to the precipice of the step, she pulled forward, scraping her chest's armour on the step. She felt no difference in height from any other; she stood. *Clearly, this was a machination of the creature, a trick of the light.* The tower now loomed over her, nowhere near as tall or wide as it seemed from the Hamlet, but almost house-sized. *Yet more trickery.* She thought to herself.

Looking to the ground for any sign of the beast she hunted, a Strange claw-like mark drew her eyes forward, following the cold stone walls of the tower, each mark consisting of three scratches to the front and a gouge at the rear. Lemma's mind twisted as she tried to decide what she saw. *The size of these claws is definitely avian, too big for anything native. What on Apprite has moved in here?* Before she could examine further, that screech from earlier filled the air above her again. Lemma's eyes darted upward, scanning the skyline for any clue that could give her even the slightest hint of what she now faced. Her mind reacted in fear. *Am I the one hunting, or am I being hunted?* Checking down at her waist, the Star began to glow brighter. *It senses it, too—what is it?*

Not a single thing flew in the eerily still blue sky; not even the clouds seemed to move. From behind the Screech came again. Lemma, flipped around, nothing but more empty air; again, behind her, the screech, but still, when she looked, just the absence of anything. Enraged Lemma called to the sky. "Whatever you are, come and face me, or are you just as cowardly as a salt weasel?" The sky remained silent; there was no response. It was as if the creature wanted the rage. Taunting her, setting her mind off balance and tenderising her thoughts into one mass of questions and fear.

"Sod this!" Lemma screamed, running for the battered and weather-worn door of the tower. Flipping the latch and smashing the door wide, she entered, greeted with the stench of blood and death, knocking her sick. Nausea filled her veins, causing her to retch and cough at the smell. Lemma reached down, pulling the kuni dagger from her waist, and cutting a long, thick strip from the base of her cloak. *This fabric smells better than the stench of this place, at least.* The thoughts flashed by as she tied the fabric at the back of her head, covering her nose and mouth—a momentary reprieve from the assault on her senses. The Star glowed brighter at her waist, warning of the taint in this place. *I already know, and I hope I can fight whatever it is.*

Taking a moment to silence the increasing fear that plagued her mind, Lemma observed the interior of the tower. It's first room square, simple wooden tables scattered about with similar in design chairs, cabinets for reports and notes on the daily watch, no windows to speak of, just slit's in the brickwork to let in daylight. *An office, by the looks of it, now where are the stairs?* Off in the far corner, she saw the stairs, almost ladder-like, not quite vertical in their alignment but sharp enough that she would need to use hands and feet to ascend them.

Climbing to the next floor was tougher than Lemma had expected. Although she could physically handle it, the muscles she used were ones she rarely used in this manner, leaving them aching and stressed from the new exercise. *By Rysand, I hope there aren't too many more floors to this tower; my arms and legs will suffer for it.* This room was simple, featuring a small stove built into the wall for cooking and ample space at the large dining table for many to eat. Lemma commented to herself. "I still don't see where that smell comes from. Is it above me?" The next set of steps further hurt the muscles.

The agony of the fibres pulling and tearing as they fought to cope left Lemma breathless. As she broke into the next room, her heart dropped. The ceiling dripped with stale, darkened blood oozing its way between the floorboards. The stench of death increased tenfold, corpses of man and fauna piled at the base of the next flight of steps. *There are at least three Scirainian soldiers in that stack. By Rysand, they will receive their burial rights, but first, I must deal with whatever beast torments this tower.*

Crossing the sticky, blood-soaked floor, she waded her way through the corpses, pulling them from her path, reeling back as she pulled an amputated arm from the pile by its hand, the upper arm torn and shredded, still wet with its owner's blood. Throwing the arm behind her, holding back the bile burning inside her throat. Lemma pulled the body of a sheep out of the way and stepped over a rib cage of some animal. Reaching up, clasping onto the fourth or fifth crimson-stained step, pulling her own body free of the carnage beneath her, she began the final ascent. Screeching cut the air above her as the remains of something fell from the gap over her head. She threw out her left arm to deflect it away. The still fresh blood flowed down her arm, still warm, hearing the bone crunch as they hit the deck below her. *It's above me; it has to be on the viewing deck.*

Peeking from the Square hole, checking the vicinity was clear, Lemma pulled up the final step, her once shiny new armour now blood-stained and aged. *Wheat sacks! The state of me, and I've not even fought yet.* Upright and on her feet, scanning the horizon, she finally saw it —the creature that played with her mind, haunting her and this place. There, perched on the edge of the viewpoint, a bird gargantuan in size, its body black and rotted feathers almost nonexistent. The skin melted and congealed, its once rounded, smooth beak a jagged mess of cracks and crevices.

It screeched, seeing Lemma facing it, flaring its immense wings, casting a shadow fifteen meters wide, launching into flight straight at her, claws raised. At the last moment possible, Lemma leapt to the left, rolling over the floor to the nearest wall. The bird flew clear out into the sky, turning back for its second attack. Scrambling for the Star, Lemma let it fly directly in the path of the bird. Spinning through the air, it flew, coming close to the bird, diving under the wing and scarring down the length of its side. The kuni blades of the Star dissecting the rotten flesh, blackened blood spewing out and down to the ground below like viscous rain, passing the rear of the bird as lightning struck, missing and hitting the wooden platform.

In swooped the bird, stabbing its beak in Lemma's direction, taking a chunk of the wall with it as it did. The Star had begun its return flight to Lemma as the bird landed opposite her on the tower. It twisted its form to face her, its claws digging into the floor. It walked, squawking, stabbing at the air, blood dripping from its wide-open wound. Steps away from Lemma, it thrust forward, aiming to take her head in one crunched motion of its battered beak. Before it could connect, the Star flew in, sawing deep into the keratin of the beak and removing the upper half from its disfigured face. Lightning struck, burning the centre mass of the bird.

Angered, it took to flight again, claws lashing out as Lemma caught the Star in time to deflect its blow away; still, the blow was strong enough to put her flat on her back. Just as quickly as Lemma could throw the Star out, the bird was back on her, its claws slamming down and destroying the wooden floor board an inch from her head. She pulled her small Kuni dagger from her waist and rolled, stabbing the blade into the bird's claw with all her strength.

An almighty Squawk of anguish came from the bird as it flapped its wings in pain and pulled itself backwards, tugging at its impaled foot. The Star reached the pinnacle of its throw, hanging there, its rate of spin increasing as a pinwheel of lightening formed around it. Suddenly crashing down, it cut into the torso of the bird, the heat of the Star searing the edges of the wound as it did. Blood hissed past its boiling point, evaporating as the Star dug slowly deeper until the bird fell dead as it cut through the centre of its ball-sized heart. Lightning struck behind it, following its path of destruction, blowing a massive hole out of the bird's chest. It covered Lemma in its thick, gummy and blackened blood, spraying forth in waves of unbridled rage unfilled.

Lemma lay there stunned in silence. *The Star acted alone to protect me without command, and with such ferocity.*

11

Slip, Trip and Fall

After descending the tower and trudging through the deluge of black and Red blood that seeped through each layer of flooring and down the mountain steps back to the Hamlet, Lemma entered the quiet, empty guest house through the small entrance room past the guest log. She ascended the rustic wooden stairs to the room she had slept in the night before. The remains of the items she had bought were carried in her arms and thrown onto the bed as she sorted them out, looking for something to change into. I need to get out of this armour, it stinks worse than a sewer rat at a Mullock dung party.

The search was proving fruitless; nothing of any real worth

was found in the first two bags: food, a couple of empty water skins, that was it. Losing hope, she would shed her outer layer. Lemma pulled the largest of the burlap sacks over, unstrapping it and tipping the contents out. As luck would have it, a pair of black leather pants and a loose-fitting black cotton shirt caught her eye. *Not what I'd usually wear, but better than nothing. Now, if only I could find a way to wash myself down.*

Clothes were found, and Lemma left the room to search for them. *Does this place have a bath? I've seen the latrine; it wasn't there, but there was that room at the back, down the wooden-walled hallway past the two other bedrooms and the door to the latrine, which was signposted with a comedic picture of a salt weasel sitting on a bowl.* There, at the back of the building, was a room she hadn't bothered to check. On its door hung a sign as odd as it was. A pig in a trough, splashing,

Lemma looked in hope. *Whomever this guest house belonged to seems to love these weird little signs. If the salt weasel was the latrine, could a pig in a trough be a bath?* Pushing the door open, there it was —a large, round plunge tub big enough for one to bathe, above it an odd little spout with a chain dangling next to it. Lemma pulled the chain. To her delight, clean, fresh water flooded from it, splashing into the tub and filling it extremely fast. *Wow, that's quite an ingenious idea. I wonder how it works? I'll tell the smarty pants back in the castle about this and see what they think.*

Looking to her left, Lemma spied a shelf unit full of jars and small hessian sacks, each labelled differently. She wandered across, reading the labels. *Essence of lavender, that's for sleep, I think. Will thyme extract stress? Peppermint relaxation, that sounds good. Byzantium rose-infused sea salt.* Upon seeing some of these ingredients, Lemma realised that this guest house was a little more refined than just a backwater nowhere hotel; they actually catered for their guests. Selecting the jars and small sacks she wanted from the shelf, she returned to the almost full bath, shutting off the flow of water, and then added decent handfuls of the ingredients she had selected, thinking. *The water might not be as hot as the royal bath, but it's clean, and that will help me feel better.*

Disrobing and taking a towel from the other side of the room, she placed it at the bath's edge. Lemma slid into the water, her body melting into it. The smell of Peppermint and Byzantium filled her nostrils, completely aiding her to switch off—the sea salts permeating the very fibres of her muscles. The room-temperature water lapped over her body, soothing it and lulling her to sleep. *By the benevolence, this is heavenly after that.....* Her final thought faded to nothing.

****

Outside the inn, a solitary soldier approached, scanning the hamlet for any signs of Lemma, vomiting the very second he came upon the now slowly rotting remains of Lemma's horse. Recovering from the shock, he rushed inside the guest house, shouting with all the sound his voice could manage. "Princess! Princess! Are you here? Princess, please answer me."

The shout jolted Lemma from her restful waterbed, causing her to fall in and be submerged entirely. She felt the chill of the water smash into her face like a war hammer. A scream erupted from her throat, garbled by the water bubbles popping on its surface. Springing up and over the tub's edge, water splashed all over. As her feet hit the floor, the salted water's slippiness took its toll.

Lemma's feet flew into the air, passing her face as she descended towards the floor. Banging her shoulders, her head hit the deck, but the nightmare didn't stop there. The force of the fall had her skidding towards the shelf full of bath soaks and salts. Smash! She careened into it, jars and sacks tumbling down, smothering her in a rich array of perfumes and fragrances. Lemma cursed the very air itself in that moment. "Mullock's dung, what a Wheat sack I made of that. Now I smell like a strumpet in a whore house!?"

Downstairs, the soldier heard the commotion and rushed up the stairs, searching each room one by one until he found the door marked with the pig-and-trough sign. Lemma listened to the rush of footsteps, another human coming towards her, and the slip-and-slide adventure. *Curses, a person. They can't come in. I'm naked. How do I block the door?*

Lemma dove from where she knelt, using the still-slick floor to her advantage. She slid across the room, scraping her chest on the jutting out jagged splinters of wood, soon followed by those same splinters digging into her thighs. Just before the soldier attempted to open the door, Lemma made it, wedging herself against the door and firmly planting her feet with a bent knee in front of her. She screamed out. "Whoever you are! do not enter? I'm armed and lethally trained!" "Princess Lemma, is that you, Highness?" came the question from behind her outside the door.

"It is me, who are you?" Lemma called back through the wooden door of the bathroom. "I've been sent with news from Sciran. Can I please speak with you?" Asked the soldier in confusion, "Wait in the entrance room, I'll be there soon." Lemma spoke with a surge of anger, still annoyed at being disturbed and the subsequent accident. "By your command", answered the soldier, turning and marching back down the hall. Sure that the man had left, Lemma clambered to her feet. Slinging the towel around herself, she grabbed the clothing from the side, which had miraculously remained dry.

Drying off and slipping on the Soutein-gorge and briefs she had with her, she tugged on the leather pants. *Mullock's dung, these things are tight. My ass is gonna look good, though.* Jumping in place, her feet slammed down on the wooden floor. One final jump had them fully on and her foot entirely in the entrance room, dangling above the soldier's head. A tremendous gasp matched the curses that came flying from the bathroom. Lemma shoved the shirt on and called down to the soldier. "Get up here now and help me." The guard had already made his way upstairs before he heard the shout of concern. "Can I enter, Princess?" he asked, recalling that the door had remained barred the last time he stood here. "Just get your mud munching arse in here, will you?" Lemma screamed through the door, waiting for it to open. In came the guard, hardly able to contain his laughter, seeing Lemma's situation.

"Give me a hand." Lemma tried to ask politely, but her patience had already left her. "Now!" She screamed before the guard's feet could move. Scared, the guard moved as fast as humanly possible. "Can I gather you under the shoulders, Princess, so that I can lift?" He asked, worried how Lemma would respond. "How else do you expect to get me out of this damn floor?" Lemma stared straight into the guard's eyes, a full-on rage at his slow reactions. "By Rysand, hurry up, you utter salt weasel, you'll be an old man at this rate." Bent over Lemma, the guard hooked around both of her shoulders and pulled, lifting her free of the rotten floor.

"Finally, you have me free now. Fetch my stuff from the last room; it's all in there. I'll put my boots on, and then we can discuss whatever news you bring." Fully dressed, Lemma left the bathroom, passing down the hall, checking the room she stayed in, thinking. *Well, at least he followed that instruction properly.* Stood at the top of the stairs to the entrance room, Lemma bellowed. "Soldier, did you bring any coins with you? I had enough for the room, but not the repair?" The soldier stood in silence, stunned, muttering a meek reply barely hearable. "Hmm, possibly enough Princes." Lemma shook her head in disgust at herself. *This man didn't do anything. I need to be respectful; I shouldn't treat him like this.* "Soldier, I owe you an apology. I should have been kinder in my words; none of this is your fault." The soldier smiled and nodded in acceptance of the apology.

"So, to the business of why you were sent, what happens in Sciran?" Lemma had finally calmed and was able to articulate her words in a more formal and expected format. "Princess, I bear dreadful news. The city has been beset with terrible monsters, small groups attacking sporadically." The soldier cowered away, expecting an explosion of anger. "Mullock's dung, I've no horse, we will be riding together." No anger in her voice, just concern and an obvious need to leave immediately. "Yes, Princess, the horse is yours. Leave me here if you need," The soldier replied. "Stop being such a salt weasel, would you? We will ride together, I said." Lemma scolded him as she walked out of the guest house's door towards his horse. The soldier left the coin on the logbook stand, noticing that Lemma must have left it there a while ago. He added it all together and hid it under the log book's spine, then followed out into the street.

12

A Princess's Duty Decided

Long into the day, they rode. Lemma sat behind the soldier, clinging to his waist as the mare fell across the smooth green grass of the plains, heading straight for Sciran. It dawned on Lemma. *I haven't even asked his name yet. Was I really that distracted?* Lemma leaned in, tucking her head to the side of the soldier, whispering into his left ear. "I feel, sir, I have done you a great disservice. Please, may I finally know your name?" The soldier's face flushed red as he heard Lemma whisper, and the heat and moistness of her breath passed his ear, causing him to stutter his reply. "I'm Ka… Kari… Karic Pe…Karic Penrov, your majesty, I took no offence to your not asking. I am, after all, only a lowly private."

The Star at the begining

Lemma spat her following words in angered whispers. "Do not put yourself down, Karic. You are a member of the Scirainian army, whether you are a private or not. Be proud, without you, our country does not flourish." Karic remained silent, a small, almost undetectable smile forming on his face in recognition of Lemma's faith in him.

"Anyway, Karic, we are to travel for five days together. I really must know more about you, your likes, dislikes and your type." Karic noted a certain level of mischievousness in Lemma's tone, caught off guard by the implications. His response. "My Type, what could you mean, Princess? Do you mean which princess I prefer?" Karic thought that it would end the conversation, but Lemma had another idea, responding, "Oh, not at all, but let's talk more when we camp."

The following two days saw them both become fast friends. Karic provided for Lemma's every need as best he could. Of course, Lemma chastised him every time and hated being waited on, as she always did and took every opportunity to tell him so. Karic continued to ignore it all, not batting an eyelid, infuriating Lemma, who began to devise a plan to really fluster Karic. *Let's see how far I can push him, a viral young man and me alone; he's done well to ignore me so far.*

That night, Lemma set about making Karic squirm, removing the little armour she still wore, pulling the leather pants tighter to lift her bum, tearing the top three inches of the black shirt to reveal her ample breasts. Then, at each opportunity, parading past Karic, accidentally on purpose, rubbing her rear against him in some fashion, be it against his shoulder as she walked, or on the one chance she got, bending over and smacking him in the face with it by the fire. Other times, she would sit so that the crack or rip in the shirt would fall open, or she would bend over, letting it fall open within his view. Karic somehow remained stoic in defiance of her continued antics not speaking or reacting, at the sudden rush of blood to his cheeks each time he caught a fleeting glance as he turned around.

Lemma's final thought before falling to sleep was of one final scheme. *Wheat sack's Karic, you're no fun; I swear I should have broken your spirits by now, had you hanging on every word. You should be like a doe-eyed puppy by now. You infuriate me. Tomorrow, I will really push you.* The light of morning broke in their small camp on the fourth and final day of riding, and by early afternoon, they would be back in Sciran. Karic breathed a sigh of relief as he thought about it. *Princess Lemma, you truly are as bad as everyone says. All you've done is toy with me, but you have not broken me. I will see you home and then be forgettable.*

Little did Karic know, Lemma had devious machinations for their final ride. Lemma looked to the sky, reckoning it must be about the ninth bell of the morning, before she began her plan. Like before, she leaned into Karic's Left ear, a sultry tone within her whisper as she spoke. "Karic, you are such a fine, strong and virile young man. If you wanted to, you could pull me from this horse. Then take me by force, enjoy my unblemished body for all your worth and slit my throat leaving satisfied. All you need to say is you found me dead in Kymei, no one would doubt you, given the horror I fought there."

Karic froze in place, his hand gripping the reins tightly, as a full bloom of blood filled his face. Crimson with shock and embarrassment, he responded in a very unflattering way. "Princess, I know you play games with me; many men warned me of your antics. Please desist from it. Beside's you are in no way this delicate damsel you portray, I had the pleasure of seeing what you did to Khrom a few weeks ago for just being him." Lemma recoiled in horror she had been out played, instant embarrassment filled her face, as she tossed her hair to one side and audibly made the sound "hmph" before falling deathly silent. *You utter salt weasel, Karic, could you not just entertain me a bit more?*

The rest of the morning, they sat in the most profound silence, making the very air feel ten times heavier. Karic concentrated on the horizon, while Lemma sat behind him sulking, a disconsolate look over her face. The twelfth bell rang heavy in the distance as the city walls broke the dreary blue and green of the horizon. "Princess, we are here. I will see you to the castle and then return to the barracks." Lemma only responded with a grunt, still sulking.

On the approach to the city gate, the stench of days-old blood filled the air, the ground scattered with random corpses of beasts, many that Lemma had never seen, some that resembled the Kitsune and other hounds. Many were humanoid in shape, but all had one thing in common apart from being dead. They were peppered with arrows, so many that Lemma couldn't begin to count them. *What has befallen my city? Where do these beasts come from? The city's defences did a magnificent job in cutting them down.* Through the Giant iron gate, they strode on horseback, the gate guards acknowledging Karic, then dropping into a bow to greet Lemma.

At the main castle door, Lemma dismounted, bidding Karic goodbye, a not-so-cheerful look still covering her face. "Be safe, Princess." Karic left on the horse, a chuckle following him, as he saw Lemma look back at him and say. "Touchè, Karic, Touchè." Entering the castle, heading straight for the throne room, Lemma rushed, forgetting the state she was in, her clothes torn and dirty. She crashed through the throne room door, shouting. "Mother!" Catherine jumped up from the throne, alarmed, and released an unusual scream — a combination of a high-pitched Half of Lemma's name and a grunt — as she fell back into the throne, gripping at her chest, feeling like her heart might explode.

Pale and still heavy of breath, Catherine managed to speak. "Lemma, you're back. How did Kymei fare?" "Kymei was the worst

I've ever seen or fought. The creature that tormented that town was grotesque beyond compare. But that is no consequence now of what has happened here?" Nonchalantly, she answered her mother's question with one of her own, feeling it held much more importance. "Well, I'm guessing you saw the Mess outside the walls as you arrived. Creatures like that have been randomly turning up at various intervals since you left, sometimes just one, others three and five, running aimlessly at the walls, dying to the defences. It's been like a blood gnat on a Mullock's arse, really. The archers barely noticed it at first." The confusion of the events showed so clearly on Catherine's face that even a baby could understand it. The whole city had been concerned when the first creature attacked, but since then, the infrequent and tiny assaults had just gone glaringly unnoticed by the populace, since none ever made a dent in the wall. Lemma stood gazing at her Mother, the Queen of this nation and the previous wielder of the Star, her mind bemused by the statement and the fact that she seemed not to have made the connection that these were foul creatures tainted by Rycore.

Lemma posed her following question very carefully, not wanting to upset Catherine. "Mother? Why are you so unalarmed? They are the creatures this world most fears; the taint still hangs about their corpses." Catherine looked down at her from the throne, a genuine discombobulation in the air around her. "They are? No one has mentioned any concern with the ease with which they fell. I felt no need to view them; perhaps I should have." Lemma stood lost for words, shaking her head, not believing her ears. *Seriously, this is my mother; she is usually so concise and exacting in all matters. It is strange, but I feel more than she does that a change is coming.* "Mother dearest, you seem to have this all under control, but something nags at me, and I fear I must leave again." "Leave again? Why?" Catherine enquired. Lemma couldn't fully explain the feelings she had when passing the dead creatures, the sense of dread it brought her, the air thick with taint; it just felt wrong that more power would be needed and soon.

"Mother, I know it somehow, though I can't tell you why? I must go and search for more, more power, more men, something to aid in the near future." Catherine realised in that moment that Lemma had tapped into the extreme empathy she felt for all things, and she was guided in a way that she and Lemma could not fully understand. "If you feel it is so, I will bolster the defences, increase the city guards, and you, my child, will begin this search. How long do you think you will be gone, and where will you go?" As Lemma watched, the understanding crossed Catherine's face that something evil was on the precipice of arrival; gladly, she answered.

"I believe I shall search for the Echidna flame, another of the Rysender, first in our own country to see if any have even the slightest tail or advice of its whereabouts. Should that fail, I will venture into enemy territory and begin again. I should think five months at the most." Catherine smiled at Lemma. "My child, do as you wish, but if you do cross the gorge, make sure to remove all Scirainian marks, and until you can trust anyone you come to know, do not reveal more than your name," Lemma answered simply before leaving the throne room, heading for her bed chamber to change, rolling her eyes. "Yes, mother."

13

At A Quest's End

Changed and ready, Lemma left her bedchamber without rest, just donning a simple yet effective full suit of non-restrictive armour. A set that had served her for many years. So much so that it felt like a second skin; it bore no identifying marks of Sciran or of her lineage. If anything, it looked more like a set a commoner would wear; that's just how plain it was, Lemma had the thought. This set is perfect; exactly what Mum wanted me to wear if I cross the gorge —comfortable and easily removable.

Walking out the side door of the Castle, Lemma made for the stables. Just outside the castle gates and next to the Hall of Arms, the officers' quarters in Sciran. Crossing the busy street of the Castle ring to a large ornate wooden arch, atop it, two carved horses butting up nose to nose. The iron gate that hung inside the wooden beams was heavily decorated with swirls and leaves. A magnificent, fine wire horse that could only be seen in full, looking as if it galloped across it once the gate closed.

A Squire caught sight of Lemma as she entered the stable yard, running off in the opposite direction to alert the stable master of her arrival. Moments later, the squire came scurrying back, stopping a few steps away from Lemma, dropping into a very low bow, so low that Lemma chuckled and commented. "Careful, Squire, much lower and you will have your face in that horse dung below you." The young Squire went all sheepish and quiet, eyes open wide in wonderment, as he listened to Lemma speak with him and talk back.

"Thank you, Princess, you honour me by speaking to one so low of station." Lemma snarled at the boys' comment and spoke with an air of contempt. "Squire, those formalities will serve you well with others, not me. Now, please do not demean yourself in such ways, a squire is a valuable position in the army, without you, those who fight can not function." The young Squire squealed giddily just before he and Lemma heard the stable master coming from behind him.

"Let me guess, Princess, this new young squire of mine

spoke overly formally as they all do till you have scolded them once or twice." His voice was gruff yet ready, and still jovial and endearing to hear. Beaming with a joy not often seen, Lemma spoke. "Ahh, Stable master Bellaton, I see you are well and still using me to instil fear in your newest charges. Anyway, is that the way you should greet me?"

Then rushed at him, diving into his arms and nuzzling into his chest. "Bellaton, you are still as chubby as ever, all the more cuddly for it. When will we ever have time to ride together again? I miss our hacks out into the plain." The poor squire dared not move from his spot except for a stumble, seeing him step in a massive pile of horse muck that Lemma warned him of. "Boy, never you mind this, get back to your duties," Bellaton ordered, still holding Lemma close.

The Squire scuttled off to attend to his jobs, leaving Lemma and Bellaton alone. Bellaton was first to speak. "Now, Lemma, I am no longer family, you know that this improper behaviour, since your aunt left me, I have tried to stop you, but I do miss our rides as well." Lemma looked up at Bellaton, staring straight into his hazel eyes, and spoke with a condescending tone. "And since when do I have to listen to you?" Then stuck her tongue out and stamped on Bellaton's foot.

"Now, Bellaton, when you've finally finished being hopping mad." Lemma burst out in laughter at her own words, needing to take several deep breaths before she could speak again. "I need a new horse, a foul beast got my last one, but I need it to be sturdy and able to last me five months of travel." Bellaton hopped about, cursing under his breath, whilst nodding and sizing up Lemma's request. "This way, Lemma, I have the perfect companion for you, a rare white stud, taller than most, broader than all, yet still as agile as any Scirainian mare you've met." Following Bellaton quickly, they came to a large half door covering a stable entrance. Bellaton whistled and called out. "Moonmane" Above the half door appeared a pristine white horse looking out to find Bellaton, its mane silver and glittering in the sunlight, catching Lemma's eye and taking her breath away, leaving only her thoughts.

Bellaton, you salt weasel, why have I never seen him before, and that mane, I see why you call him that. Her thought finished, she spoke one word. "Mine." Bellaton nodded, "I already knew that."

Moonmane was taken from the stall, a fine yet oddly standard saddle placed on his back, and pack hooks thrown over his rump filled with necessities. Lemma jumped to his back with a gleeful smile, looked to Bellaton, said her goodbyes and rode out of the stables, speaking directly into her new mount's ear. "Moonmane, you replace a fine mare who served me well for many a year. I hope you ride smoothly. I need no saddle saws."

Through the city's streets, prancing away, Moonmane carried her, carefully and reliably, until the iron gates. There, his more feral senses kicked in, jarring in his step, eager to run. Almost as Lemma felt his immense emotion wanting to run free, she leaned to his ear and whispered. "Moonmane, should we go?" Without a second thought, Moonmane Sprinted out of the iron gate, clipping a guard and spinning him in place. Lemma called back. "Sorry", Moonmane ran free, only changing direction with a prompt of the reins. His speed was easily twice that of any mare Lemma had ridden before.

Two uneventful days sailed past in the blink of a cat's eye, and Lemma was back in Ashreb. For three weeks, she pored over the old tomes and diaries of Lord Favener's family, gleaning only one small hope from any of them, a statement in an ancient, almost entirely dilapidated diary. The words on the page were not fully clear to anyone who read them. *The Echidna Flame is held by.* Then the words became muddy and illegible until the end of the page, where more writing was added. *The general will return at the time of great need.*

During the three-week stay, she had studied these tomes. Lemma had seen that Nyrina was almost fully recovered and would soon be able to return to Sciran. However, she also saw something else, which led to her dismissing Nyrina from her service, much to Nyrina's dismay, and subsequently placing her as Princess Faith's personal guard. Nyrina and Faith had grown beyond the closeness of friends in the recent days, and it was clear to see they were more. Lemma thought about it in depth. *I wish them both well. I will not see such pure love splintered by my hand. Sorry, Nyrina, you may be my friend, but Faith is my sister, and you are hers more than mine now.* After settling all issues arising from the service transfer, with Faith and Nyrina's approval. Sitting on Moonmanes' back, Lemma left Ashreb, heading south along the mountains towards Kymei point, where she planned to verify that everything was back to normal.

The journey South saw Lemma stopping in many small villages and towns over the next four weeks, questioning the locals to no avail; her quest seemed to lead nowhere, except across the gorge in hopes of more information. Eventually, midway through the eight weeks, she entered Kymei again. Tethering Moonmane at the guest house, she entered, and this time, a frail old lady greeted her wide-eyed and smiling. "Hello, dear, how can I help?" the old lady asked. Lemma smiled and replied. "I came via this guest house while you all evacuated to Dracklow fort, simply I came to apologise for the mess and see that my payment covered the cost."

The lady immediately realised who stood before her and spoke formally. "Princess, welcome, thank you for the visit indeed, the coin left covered the repairs and more." Lemma nodded, thanked the lady for the news, and left, thankful that at least some good came of the carnage she left behind last time she visited.

Onward from Kymei she rode. Six days of endless riding finally brought her to the Ryecliff bridge, where crossing it took almost a full day's ride. On the other side, she spoke with a traveller, who gave her directions to Lehoi, the biggest town near the bridge.

A further half-day's ride brought her to Lehoi. Renting a room at the local tavern for nearly three weeks, she heard that the Ryecliff bridge had collapsed just hours after her arrival, severing the rope that had once marked the boundary between Occardian and Ryecliff lands. Lemma tried to gather yet more information.

Unsuccessful, she resorted to persistence and staying in Lehoi until her room rental ended, despite being fed up with the local men ogling her and constantly making comments about how she would be in their bed before she left. Then the very masculine approach to the legends of Rysand and Hagen—the first King of Occard after the war—also irritated her so much.

Lemma took the time to play their little games, enticing them to the point they would make advances, forceful or otherwise, then taking great pleasure in pulverising them to within an inch of their lives. The local watch always arrived after the shenanigans had finished and ended up dragging the unconscious man away after many witnesses reported that Lemma had only defended herself.

The end of her stay soon came, fruitless and without reward; she left informed of a farming village by the name of Grissam, about two hours away, where rumours had been of strange occurrences within the last decade.

A quick visit, but I doubt I'll find anything useful. All the same, it's worth a try. I have time to kill; the bridge is still a week away from repair. Into Grissam she rode, meeting with locals hearing of the horrific plague that took the Crown prince too soon and the strange death of the previous king. Little did these people know, Lemma knew more about these situations than she dared even reveal. *Mother, you were right to imprison that vile man; these people will one day see the truth.*

She learned nothing in Grissam and moved farther west until she reached a final village, where she was told there were no towns beyond it.

The return to Lehoi would take seven days. Only Moonmane for company on the dusty, unforgiving roads of the grasslands, Lemma spent some of that lost in conversation with Moonmane; most would have thought her a little on the mad side as she spoke solely to a horse. Recounting her years spent in the saddle of her previous mount.

"Moonmane, you never met your predecessor, but I think you two would have got on. If you had met, I can only imagine the foal you two could bear. Your stunning silvery mane mixed with her fiery auburn coat. She had the speed of a gale at her back; the wind seemed to flow with her, and her movements felt like floating along a gently roving river. That's not to say you're rough, your speed is awe-inspiring, and you ride like the storm chases you." Moonmane seemed to understand her sentiment, greeting her with contented snorts. Lost in the one-sided conversation, Lemma continued.

"I remember this one time, we leapt a brook, she lost her footing on the landing, but rather than see me wet, she somehow twisted in such a way that she landed sideways onto the brook's bank, me hanging from the stirrups, upside down in a heather patch, which she then promptly ate. I think she liked the taste, as for days after she kept trying to eat my hair until the heather's scent faded away."

It was almost as if Moonmane laughed at the image as he neighed with glee. These odd little conversations with Moonmane continued. Each day, Lemma travelled closer to Lehoi, and she would spend time reminiscing about all things, recounting how she had eaten the repeaters' stew under the city, even splitting Gruladans' Wheat sacks in two.

Over the seven days passing, Lemma had grown exponentially more fatigued; still, Lemma had no intention of staying and passed on through Lehoi as it came and left her view. Daylight was still on her side as she pulled up to a riverbank, letting Moonmane drink. Lemma knelt at the river's edge, removing her helmet so she could wash her face and drink, tucking her auburn hair to the side and making a cup with her hand. She cupped the water to her mouth more easily. As she drank, the Star began to glow at her waist. Lemma looked up towards the far riverbank, from there came numerous harsh forms of men, barely even containing the souls of men anymore, half-formed curses and shouting, assaulting her ears.

Into the waters of the river they plunged, jagged, slow steps, stumbling on river rocks, disappearing under the river's surface, reappearing and surrounding her. Weapons raged above their head, ready to attack. Lemma stood, placing her helmet back on her head, and removed the Star from her waist; its glow intensified.

A swift flick of her wrist, the Star set loose, carving through the air at the first man. Slicing through an arm, then dipping for the next few, it separated legs from hips. On its final assault, decapitating her many attackers, red crimson blood spurted forth in fountains, soaking the earth, as the rivers' water ran red. Lightning crashed down, burning the ground all around them. Her thought wandered; the Star didn't return. *What on Apprite? Why won't it return?*. Watching as the Star zipped past, her heading behind her over the grass at the riverbank. Careening towards a solitary man stood under a tree, her mind still thinking as he stood in silence, awaiting this minion of Rycor's death and the Stars' return to her hand. Crash, the sound of Metal on metal filled the air as blue lightning struck the tree next to this man, and the Star fell to the floor. Lemma stood there, awe-struck, thinking. *He stopped the Star, how?*

A note from the Author

Hi, I hope you enjoyed reading this short novella, which briefly recounts the history of Lemma, the Female Main Character from the main book, The Jade Pandora Two Kings, One Throne. The first book in The Jade Pandora Saga,

Now I'll be heading back to writing the second book in The Jade Pandora saga and preparing it for release in 2026, and hoping to see you back in Apprite very soon.

Thanks again for reading this. Please take a moment to review this book on Goodreads or any other book review site of your choice. It would mean a great deal to me. I had a great time writing the novella, and I hope you enjoyed learning about Lemma's past as much as I did writing it for you.

A.D Stevens

This QR code will take you to the internet home of The Jade Pandora.

Printed in Dunstable, United Kingdom

71145316R00071